A House Made of Stars

A House Made of Stars

A NOVEL BY

Tawnysha Greene

PUBLISHED BY

Burlesque Press

Published by Burlesque Press
www.burlesquepressllc.com

Excerpts have been published in the following magazines:

*The Variety Show, storySouth, Blue Lake Review, JMWW, PANK
Magazine, A-Minor, Monkeybicycle, Waccamaw, Staccato Fiction, 52/250 A
Year of Flash, Eunoia Review, Rougarou: An Online Journal, Cutthroat: A
Journal of the Arts.*

ISBN: 978-0-9964850-0-5

Set in Adobe Garamond

Book design by Daniel Wallace

For Grandma

ONE

Momma tells us it's a game.

She pulls back our bed covers, grabs hold of our nightgowns, and pulls me and my sister into the hallway. Momma's in her pajamas, too, and I stumble against the light and Momma's feet in front of mine. All the lights in the house are on.

I hear noise even though I'm hard of hearing, dull thuds that sound at the other end of the house. I look back, but Momma jerks me forward, tells me to hurry.

We go to the only place that's still dark. The bathroom at the end of the hallway, the small one where there's a window and the shower curtain is lace, not plastic like it is in the bigger one. She pulls us inside and shuts the door behind us, locks it, and keeps the light off.

She smiles at us and puts a hand to her lips, like she's told us a secret. Motioning to the towels, Momma pulls them off the rack and sets them in the tub, makes us climb in, and she drapes more on top of us. I feel the thuds again, only in the sides of the tub, and my sister feels them, too. She's completely deaf, but the vibrations in the house are ones we all sense and know.

Momma signs to us.

"We're practicing," she signs, "for an earthquake." Her sign for the last word is big as she makes the word for earth, then clenches both hands into fists and beats the air in front of her.

Light comes in from underneath the door behind her, and

we can see that her face is animated, her eyes big, and my sister laughs. I want to laugh, too, but I am distracted by Momma's fists in the air, her small, pale knuckles, because I think of the other fists at the end of the house where our earthquake is, where Daddy is.

Momma gets in the tub, and pulls the lace shower curtain closed, and it's even darker than it was before. She sits down between us, and we lean on her as she puts her arms around us. She continues to sign, her hands farther apart, shadows now against the muted lights from the underneath the doorway, but we can still see what she says.

"If we hide in the tub," she signs, "it will keep us safe if the walls come down."

I remember the lessons from the library book we got not long ago. The book's cover was worn and some of the pages were missing, but she read it to us during school time, told stories about fires, storms, and safety.

I don't tell her that she's wrong about the earthquakes, and that hiding in the tub was only for tornadoes. I don't want her hands to stop, because she doesn't sign to us a lot anymore, instead she talks to us with her mouth instead, like Daddy does.

We lie against her and try to fall asleep as she signs above us. She tells us how to hide if the earthquake lasts a long time, what to do if the house falls down around us.

Two

The shower curtain is open when I wake up, and Momma's gone. The bathroom door is ajar. It's morning.

The house smells of cleaning sprays and Pine-Sol, and when I peek down the hallway, the carpet is vacuumed. All the windows are open. In our room, our beds are stripped, our dressers emptied, the drawers still out, and our pillows taken away.

Momma told us about today, the day movers would come and take back our rental furniture and then we would move to a hotel, one by the Los Angeles airport where the rent was cheap. She told us this a month ago when Daddy lost his job.

In the living room, our things are gathered in boxes, our clothes in suitcases, and our pillows stacked by the door. Momma's in the kitchen, and my sister is there, too. They both wear yellow rubber gloves as they kneel and scrub the cabinets and the knobs on the doors.

I look for where the sounds came from last night, but Daddy's gone, and Momma's cleaned everything to be as it was before. Everything looks perfect.

Momma sees me and tells me to hurry. They'll be here soon.

They'll take the couch, the big-screen TV, our nightstands, the red bunk bed my sister and I share, and the table in the dining room. Yesterday, we gave back all our library books. The day before that, we gave the neighbors our plants.

With the refunded security deposit the landlord will give us after his inspection today, we'll be set to stay at the hotel for ten days and have extra for food. Momma says that'll give Daddy enough time to get another job, and then, we'll move again.

Momma has tricks she knows, and she teaches us how to color in scratches on the furniture with a marker the same color, fill in nail holes in the wall with white toothpaste, and rub Pine-Sol on the baseboards to make the house smell extra clean.

The movers are here before we're ready, and Momma tells us to get dressed. The movers talk to each other as they load the dressers and the nightstands and wrap bright straps around the furniture, so that nothing falls when they roll everything up the ramp into their truck. They have to disassemble our bed, and my sister and I watch them take off the mattresses and unscrew the frame.

One of the guys looks strong like Daddy, his shirt wet with sweat despite the January cold outside, and I watch the way his hands are quick with the tools, but gentle with the bed as he takes the pieces apart. He waves at us and asks our names.

I'm not expecting the question, and I stare at him and pull my sister closer. I sign to her that we need to find Momma, and we turn to the hallway, but two of the other movers are in our way. They're carrying a dresser, and it blocks the hallway. I stare at the floor. "How old are you?" the same man asks.

He doesn't sound like Daddy. His voice is calm.

"Ten," I say, not looking at him.

The men move the dresser forward, and the hallway is clear again.

4

My sister runs to where Momma is talking to a mover holding a clipboard. I wait a moment, then look back at the man who looks strong like Daddy. He smiles, and I wonder if he is a dad, too.

"My sister's six."

Momma motions me to the kitchen and to the list on the counter. I open the package of magic erasers, wet them and hand one to my sister, and we start working on the walls. The landlord comes when we're halfway through.

I've only seen him once when a pipe broke under the kitchen sink, but he looks the same—dressed in a button-down shirt and jeans, hair pulled back in a ponytail, his face tired and haggard as he itches behind his ear and blows air out of his mouth while stepping inside. He walks with Momma through the rooms, and my sister and I hurry as fast as we can as we clean the refrigerator, dust the window blinds that still won't close all the way, and begin mopping the floor.

We scrub the sink with Comet that makes it shine, take out the eyes of the stove and wash underneath, and soon, everything looks better than it ever did before. My sister and I take off our gloves and set them with all the other cleaning supplies, then dry our arms.

But they never come in the kitchen to see what we've done. The landlord is shaking his head when he heads to the door, and Momma follows behind.

"Please," she says. "We need this money."

He points down the hallway where the carpet is ripped, to the dent in the wall where Daddy hit it when he lost his job. His voice is loud when he tells Momma, no.

Momma watches him walk away and continues to stand there in the open doorway as his car speeds down our street and toward the highway. The moving men are gone, and the rooms are empty, indentations in the carpet where the rental furniture was before.

She sits and covers her face with her hands.

The air feels cold as it comes in through the doorway, and I put the cleaning supplies in a big bag. We don't need them anymore.

My sister sits next to Momma, and Momma puts an arm around my sister's shoulders. I sit next to her, too, and we wait for our van to come up the driveway, and for Daddy to step out.

When he does, he's in the same clothes as he was last night before we went to bed, jeans and a flannel shirt with the sleeves rolled up past his forearms. He wears a black Raiders cap. He leaves the van door open—he's ready to leave.

Momma gets up and wipes her face.

Daddy comes inside, and she goes to the kitchen and pretends to clean, but everything's been done. She opens and closes cabinets, and turns on the water, turns it off, then on again. She doesn't say anything.

"You ready?" he asks, and he takes up our suitcases and our pillows until his arms are full.

Momma comes out from the kitchen. She starts to say something, then stops and cries again.

Then, he knows.

His breath comes out slow. I don't hear it, but I see his chest go down in one long moment as his jaw juts out, his mouth only slightly open. He blinks slow, his motions measured, almost methodical as he sets down one suitcase, then the other, then pauses. He tenses then throws everything left in his arms—the pillows, the blankets—throws them down until everything is scattered on the floor.

He takes a step back, his hands tense as they come up near his face. His teeth clench and his eyes get smaller as he holds his head slightly to the side. The burn scar, one that runs from his hand to his neck and the side of his left ear, darkens the way it does when he's angry. He turns and yells as he heads down the hallway, and Momma runs to the door where my sister and I are watching and pushes the suitcases toward us.

She tells us to go to the van.

We grab the pillows, too, as much as we can carry and rush outside. Momma comes out with the rest and helps us open the back and put everything inside. We get in our seats, and Momma leans over us. In her hands are the keys.

"Stay here," she says. "I have to take care of Daddy."

She leaves, locks the doors. We wait until nightfall. I'm asleep when we leave and when I wake up, it's cold. Snow is falling outside, and the road is steep and curvy.

We aren't going to the hotel, but I know where we are.

THREE

We haven't been up this mountain since Daddy's momma died last year, but it's where he used to live as a boy.

Daddy drives fast, and I feel the pull of each bend in the road. He goes around the trucks ahead, and Momma holds on to the handle on the door until he slides back into the right lane. It's hard to see. The defroster is broken, and the windshield is fogged. Daddy sticks his head outside, and the snow comes in, melts on his hair, the seat, and on us. My sister's asleep. It's after midnight.

When we reach the street where Daddy's sister lives, the houses are dark. We stop at the gray one with the white trim, the chain-link fence, and a black oak tree. That one is dark, too.

Momma gets out, and Daddy turns off the car. Momma knocks on the door, but no one comes. She knocks again, then again, and a light comes on in the kitchen. Daddy's sister comes to the door. She's in a bathrobe, and she shades her eyes from the porch light. I see the curtains move upstairs where my cousin looks out, her hands against the window.

Momma and Daddy's sister hold hands, and Momma points to the car, to us, and Daddy's sister nods, motions us to the house, to the light inside.

When they open the car door, I pretend I'm just waking up. Momma picks up my sister, and I follow them up the driveway, the ice slick under my feet, and my breaths come out of my mouth like clouds. A fire burns in the wood stove, and Daddy's sister gets sheets from the linen closet and puts them on the floor. We stuff pillows in cases that smell of lavender, and I hold them to my face to breath it in. It's the same laundry soap Momma uses.

"I'm sorry," Momma says.

Daddy's sister shushes her. "It's okay."

Daddy's still outside, and through the window, I can see his shadow on the porch, pacing like he did at home. His hand goes up through his hair and then down again as he turns and walks the other way.

Daddy's sister watches, too. He hasn't said a word to her.

"When we didn't get the money, we didn't know what else to do," says Momma as she spreads the sheets and blankets on the floor.

Daddy's sister puts a hand on Momma.

"How long?" she asks, and Momma looks out the window, too.

Momma takes in a breath.

"Three days."

I know they're talking about Daddy, but I don't ask them why, because I know if I do, they'll stop.

"He's usually okay by now," says Momma.

Daddy's sister takes the sheets and blankets where Momma left them and finishes making a bed on the floor. Her hands are quick and sure. "He'll be alright," she says. "Best thing is just to stay out of his way."

Momma's voice gets quiet, and I have to read her lips to see what she says.

"It scares me."

Daddy's sister's hands pause on the sheets. "I know."

They don't say anything for a moment, then Daddy's sister nods toward the top of the stairs.

"I think she's asleep," she says, and I think of my cousin upstairs at the window. Momma lays her things on the floor where she and Daddy will sleep, then takes my sister and me up the stairs.

As we reach her room, my cousin's bed creaks. The nightlight is on, blankets hastily cast over her form, and then I see why—the floor vent by the foot of her bed is pulled out, lying on its side where her face had been moments before. She had shown me how she did this the last time we were here, a butter knife slipped underneath the side and pulled up until the vent came free. It was after Daddy's momma's funeral, and while our mothers sat downstairs, we watched them eat bread and lasagna, and listened to them talk.

Momma takes a blanket from Daddy's sister's room and sets it by my cousin's bed. She kisses us then goes back down the stairs, and we wait until her shadow is gone, and my cousin climbs out of bed. We crowd near the vent, our skin and hair touching, as we had done after the funeral. Their voices are low, and it's hard to hear, and my cousin signs what they say, so that my sister can understand. Daddy's momma was deaf, too, and that's why my cousin knows sign, to talk to her when Daddy's momma lived with them before she died.

Momma's crying now. "I just want to help him."

"You are," says Daddy's sister. "Just be there for him when he comes back down. He'll need you."

My cousin's signs are soft, her fingers gentle as they slide from one word to the next. When Daddy's sister says, "you," my cousin points to my sister and to me.

I wait for Momma to talk about the last time he didn't sleep, the days and nights that stretched into something that seemed like it wouldn't end, but my cousin's hands are still, the house quiet as we listen through the vent.

Daddy's sister tells Momma to stay as long as we need.

They go to bed and turn off the lights, and we put the vent back. My sister and I lie down, still in our clothes, and my cousin gives us another blanket from the closet to share. It's a quilt with pink squares, torn along the side, and as everyone falls asleep, I stare at the stars on the ceiling, stickers that shine in the dark. My cousin put them up years ago, showed me the stars when we stood on her bed as her fingers traced over the outlines, and then she turned out the lights, so that I could see them glow.

Four

In the morning, snow speckles the windows. The snowplow hasn't come by yet, and when I look out the window, the streets are smooth with whiteness. Daddy's shoveling the driveway, making a path from the street to the front door. He doesn't wear a jacket or gloves and from the distance, I can see his hands pink in the cold. Momma said that he likes the cold—that's why he runs the air in the wintertime, sleeps with no blankets on.

Downstairs, Daddy's sister sets dishes on the table and tells Momma what's new since the last time we visited—the restaurant by the stoplight and the walkway by the lake. I glance down the stairs. My sister's pouring cereal in blue plastic bowls, standing on her chair, leaning over the table to pour milk from a yellow jug.

The door to the bathroom creaks, and my cousin peeks out, motions me in. She stands in front of the mirror, and I sit on the side of the bathtub, watching her curl her hair, like I used to watch Momma at home. Momma calls these moments "special time," a phrase her mother used when Momma was a girl and Grandma washed Momma's face, braided her hair, licked her palms, and smeared them over Momma's hair to keep the strays down, things Momma does to us, too.

My cousin does her hair differently than Momma does, curls under in the back, pins, sprays down the sides, her fingers delicate, gentle, like the way she signs. She puts aloe vera on her face and arms, green gel that makes her skin gleam. She takes my hand, hers still sticky, and pulls me in front of the mirror.

The sink is cluttered with brushes and combs on each side of the faucet. She gives me her brush, a round one full of her hair, and I look in the mirror, pull it through mine, hold the top of my head when I reach tangles, like I had seen her do. She watches me, turns the sink faucet on, cups water in her hands, then drips it over my head.

She takes the brush, does the back, twists my hair, pulls and ties it with a pink band. Her nails are pink, too, and I put my hand up to hers to see the design, pink on one side, white on the other, a line in between.

"How'd you do that?"

She gets a pencil from the shelf and shows it to me.

The lead is marked with nail polish, stained white and pink, purple and black from times before.

"Want me to do yours?"

I nod, hold out my hand, and she gets the nail polish and sits on the floor. She draws the lines on my nails, presses down hard, marking where polish will go. Daddy's sister calls from downstairs, and my cousin yells back, eyes not moving from her work.

We're leaving soon for church, the one Daddy's sister goes to past the frozen lake, the ski slopes on the other side of the mountain. I remember cassettes of the sermons Daddy's sister mailed Momma. Momma listened to them when she did the dishes in the mornings, sometimes right after we went to our own church, and while my sister and I played under the dining table, pretending we were wolves hiding in a den, the pastor's voice talked, every word drawn out.

My cousin paints my nails, her fingers sure as she curves her wrist, stops, then wipes when the paint reaches skin. The polish is cold, but her hands are warm. Daddy's sister calls again.

My cousin doesn't move, but closes one bottle of nail polish, opens another. She paints with pink now, covers some of the white, the pencil line underneath. She blows on it to dry, and her breath feels strange on my skin.

She puts the polish away.

"You think your dad will come?"

"To church?" I ask. "No."

Daddy's sister calls again. Neither of us answer.

"Does he like God?"

"I don't know," I say.

I know his momma taught him prayers, ones he said as he knelt, touched his head, chest, and shoulders when he and Daddy's sister crossed themselves after she died. At her funeral, their mouths moved as one, said the same words, too quiet for me to understand, but I knew they said them often when they were children, their movements timed, memorized, done without thinking.

During the funeral, I never looked at the urn that held her ashes or the man in a robe who blessed it and absolved her of things he would not name. I stared only at the way Daddy and his sister moved together, spoke at certain times, then when it was over, took her ashes from the altar, and carried them to the graveyard. Neither of them cried when she was put into the ground and when the man prayed again, sent her soul to God, they bowed their heads again, whispered, Amen.

Five

Daddy's gone when we go outside, our van's tire tracks fresh in the snow on the street, so we all take Daddy's sister's car to church. Her car is smaller than ours and smells of cinnamon, and I see a red tree hanging from her rearview mirror. She drives like Daddy, one hand on the wheel, but waves to people she passes by, unlike him.

I look for him as we drive down their street, past the big hotel where Daddy's sister works, and toward the part of town Daddy's sister called The Village. A lot of cars are covered with snow, the side windows dusted, so it's hard to see inside, but I search for Daddy's sharp nose, thin lips, his eyes under a heavy brow. I don't see him anywhere.

He's still gone when we get home from the church service, and Daddy's sister takes us to the room above her garage, the room she had built when Daddy's momma came to live with her before she died. The walls are different now, Daddy's momma's framed prayers and crucifixes gone, but the room still smells of pine and her—a familiar scent of honey and cigarette smoke.

The last time I was in this room was when I sat on the floor as Daddy's momma poured jelly beans in a bowl, picked out the pink ones she liked best and gave them to my sister and me. She and Momma sat at the table in the kitchen and talked while my sister and I played with the wicker basket at the foot of her bed, the old telephones and plastic pearls inside.

16

I look for these things, pieces of his momma that may have been left behind, but the room is swept clean. The windowsills are dusted, the sink and bathtub scrubbed, and the nail holes in the walls filled in. Her rocking chair, the television that clicked with each turn of the channel, and the bowls of jelly beans are gone.

I wonder if that's why Daddy's not here—that he didn't want to come. He never went in this room. The week before his momma died, Momma and Daddy's sister took turns going up the stairs to see her. Momma left us in Daddy's sister house, but Daddy always stayed outside, standing for hours on the icy driveway, hands in his pockets, breathing in the cold. Sometimes, Momma or Daddy's sister would come down from the room, ask him if he wanted to see her, but from what I could see as I watched from the window, he never turned or said anything.

No one says anything now, and I wonder if Momma and Daddy's sister are thinking of her, too. Daddy's sister gives us sheets to put on the bed, and we put them on quietly. It's the only piece of furniture in the room now, other than a recliner. The room is small, and I count nine big steps wide across the room, fourteen steps long. The sink and refrigerator are on one wall, bed on the other, and a bathroom with a door that's too short at the end of the room.

There's a card table folded up by the refrigerator, and Momma gets it out and sets it up with two chairs in the middle of the room. She tells us it's where we'll have school time. She and Daddy will share the bed, and my sister and I will sleep on the floor with the blankets and pillows Daddy's sister gives us. We set them up under the window that looks out to Daddy's sister's house, and I see my cousin's room where we were the night before. My breath fogs the glass.

When the fog clears, I see the mountains beyond the forest in front of Daddy's sister's house, the peaks jagged and bright in the sun. I don't know the names of the mountains, only that our home where we used to live is beyond it, down the winding roads to the red valley where the ground is dry and cracked, where boulders big as houses stand in the sun. Our house was in the city beyond the valley, past the airfield, and stood at the end of a street. There were lots of windows, but we always kept them closed. The window my sister and I shared in our bedroom was one of the smallest in the house, but when Momma told us stories before bed, I remember the way the light from the street lamp would still come through the window blinds and cast shadows on our beds.

I miss Momma's stories. She hasn't told us any since Daddy lost his job. She says her mind is on other things, but I remember when she would kneel by our beds and tell us about girls and boys who walked through magical gardens, ones where the flowers were alive, who guided them on their way. My favorite is the story of a girl who found a magic shed in her backyard that took her to a land far from her own, where the flowers stayed open at night, the moon was always out, and the clouds never covered the stars.

Six

The sky is still dark when Momma wakes us up. She puts on our coats over our pajamas, and we step in our shoes at the front door. We go outside, and before Momma can close the door, I see Daddy asleep on the bed. I never saw him come in.

We go to the grocery stores, still closed, but Momma leaves us in the car and puts coins in the newspaper stands until the front comes open, and she reaches inside. We read through them all morning. My sister and I look for the cartoon pages, but they aren't there. It's a smaller newspaper than the one Daddy used to get at our old house. This one is thin and has a bear printed on the front page.

Momma looks through the back pages and marks things with a black pen, and I start to read them, too. Job advertisements. Momma circles them all.

I don't know what Daddy did at his old job, except that he was always tired, and we had to leave him alone when he got home. His hands were rough from his work, scabs from old wounds on his knuckles and fingers, but he never seemed to feel them, his head propped on his thumb and forefinger as he watched the evening news.

I try to picture him doing the jobs Momma circles. Delivery Driver. Billing Clerk. Server. Momma circles another. Dog washer. I stifle a laugh.

Momma looks at me, then back to the paper, hiding a smile

of her own.

"I know," she says.

We both read through the classifieds now, and I help Momma pick out more. Snow Plow Driver. Loader Operator.

"Why can't we do some of these things?" I ask. "I can wash dogs."

"They want adults, baby."

"You are an adult," I say, then hold my breath. Momma doesn't like it when I ask questions.

She closes the newspaper. "But who would teach you? Who would watch you all day?"

"We could go to school here. We could take the bus like her. You wouldn't even have to drive." My cousin could help watch out for us. She is taller and stronger than me.

"No, baby. You couldn't all be together." I don't know if she is talking about my sister or my cousin, but it's true. My cousin is twelve. My sister is six. We'd probably be in different schools.

"Besides," she says. "They don't teach Godly things there. They don't even pray."

Momma opens the newspaper again, and I lean back in my seat. Momma turns over the pages quicker now, her motions less gentle.

"I'm sorry, Momma," I say, but I don't know if she hears.

I never mention it again, and we do the same thing next week and the week after that. We wait until the newspaper boy fills up the newsstands, takes the old newspapers away, and Momma goes to them with her coins.

The newspapers stay on the kitchen counter where Momma leaves them open for Daddy, the circles around the job listings bigger and bigger with each week, but the pages go untouched. We use Momma's emergency money to get food at the store, and Momma asks the cashiers if they are looking for someone to work. The answer is always no.

On the day the newspaper boy is late and doesn't come at his regular time, we head back home, and there is a new car in the driveway. It's one we know.

It's Grandma, Momma's momma, and we can see her at the front door of Daddy's sister's house. Grandma's talking to my cousin. She turns when we pull in and her hands go up, her voice high and loud as she runs down the front steps and comes to our car.

She hugs Momma first, and Momma's hands quickly fold over the newspaper and stuff it in her back pocket before she hugs her back.

"What are you doing here?"

"I wanted to see you," she says, then she turns to us and puts her hands up in the air again. "And I had to see my babies."

She rocks us from side to side as she hugs us, and her sweater is soft against my face. She kisses us and when we kiss her back, she squeals, and hugs us again. She feels warm, and I can tell she hasn't been outside long.

"What are you all doing outside in your pajamas?" she asks us. "It's cold."

Momma gives us the keys and tells us to get dressed and then come back.

"But be quiet," she says, and she puts a finger to her lips, so my sister understands.

"I want to see your new place," says Grandma, and she starts to follow us, but Momma catches her sleeve.

"He's sleeping. I don't want to wake him," says Momma. "He's been working a lot lately."

I don't hear what else Momma tells her, but when I take my sister up the stairs to the room above the garage, we dress quickly. Daddy's still asleep, and I shove the old newspapers on the counter into a drawer. I pile everyone's dirty clothes in the closet, take down the drying clothes we had washed in the bathtub, and spread the food in the refrigerator on different shelves, so it looks like we have more. Momma always did the same things when Grandma would see us at our old house.

Momma and Grandma are waiting for us in the car, and we spend the day at the park. It's cold, but Grandma plays with us, climbs on the jungle gym, and goes with us down the slides. There's a Tic-tac-toe board on the edge of a swinging bridge, and she teaches us how to play, her hands turning over the tiles to show an X or an O. Momma watches us from the other side of the playground, and Grandma asks me questions between each turn.

Where is Daddy working. Where was Daddy yesterday. Where is Daddy now.

Her voice gets lower every time she says, "Daddy," and I know it's because she doesn't like him.

I don't know what to say, so I don't answer her, and eventually, she stops asking. Momma gathers us back in the car, and we spend all day driving around town. We point out where our cousin goes to school, where the ski slopes are, and the campgrounds where sometimes, people see bears.

Momma drives to our church, and there are already a lot of cars there. It's the Wednesday night service, and Momma gets us out and herds us to the front door.

We've never been to church with Grandma before, and my sister and I show her how we raise our hands when we sing the slow songs, clap and dance in the aisles like the other people do when the songs go fast and repeat over and over again. She laughs when we try to pull her out to the aisle to dance, too.

When the last worship song ends, the pastor asks who is new, and my sister and I raise Grandma's hand, and she tries to keep it down. The pastor sees her and asks her to stand up, and she does while another song plays and people come to greet her while she casts glances down at us, smiles, and shakes her head.

After everyone has hugged her and shaken her hand, the pastor gets up again and tells us that a guest is speaking today. A woman stands in the front row.

I look to Momma.

We've only left church in the middle of a service twice, both at churches we went to before we came to the mountains, once when the pastor said that we should love one another, even the homosexuals, a word forbidden at home, and another when the pastor's wife stood up to pray, something Momma said a woman had no right to do.

Momma stands, and we leave.

On the way back, Grandma asks why we left, and Momma

is quiet, but Grandma won't let it go. Grandma gets angry and starts to talk at the window, pausing and twisting her mouth to the side when Momma still doesn't answer.

"I don't want to expose them to that," Momma finally says.

"To what?" asks Grandma. "To a woman speaking?"

"It isn't right."

We pull into Daddy's sister's driveway, but no one gets out.

They talk for a long time, and it gets cold in the car. Momma asks Grandma to leave, and she does. She kisses us goodbye, her voice now sad, and that night, I think about the things they said in the car, about everything Grandma said a woman could be and everything Momma said a woman could not.

Seven

My cousin tells me what she and Grandma spoke of the next time I see her. We're washing the dishes after we had dinner at Daddy's sister's house, and we each stand over the sink—she's washing, I'm rinsing. Her hands are sudsy, and she's careful with the dishes, her grip strong as she gives them to me, letting go only when I am holding them with both hands.

"She asked where you were, if you were okay," she says. "She seemed worried."

I set the rinsed dishes on a towel spread out on the counter. "She asked me questions, too."

She hands me the last plate then drains her side of the sink.

"Mom says your grandma doesn't like your dad," she says. "Mom wanted me to lie, say you all weren't here."

"I'm glad you didn't lie." I drain my side of the sink, too, and rinse it out. "That would have worried her more."

We dry our hands.

Daddy and his sister are talking about Grandma, too. Their hands look the same, clenching and unclenching. They both lean forward when they talk, their eyes hard and focused on each other when they speak. Their words to describe her are the same. Nosy, judgmental, negative.

Momma looks at the ground.

"She always has to find something wrong," says Daddy, and when he speaks, he looks everywhere, talks to the entire room.

"She's always poking her head where it doesn't belong. Nothing is good enough for her."

"She won't come back. You're okay. You'll make it here," says Daddy's sister. "You don't need her."

Daddy continues the conversation to Momma, to my sister and me when he takes us to the drive-in theater later that night. He talks to himself, and tells Momma all the same things he did before.

Momma reclines our seats and tells us to sleep. "Daddy just needs to clear his mind," she says.

We did this before, got up in the middle of the night to go to the movies when Daddy was stressed, but the theater where our old house was wasn't a drive-in. It had rows of seats that smelled of popcorn, and floors that were sticky with dried soda. Momma would tell us to sleep then, too, and to not watch the movies, because they were for Daddy, not for us to see. We couldn't enjoy them anyway. Daddy talked through those movies, too.

He hits the steering wheel as he talks. "We need to get out of here. Somewhere where she can't go, where she won't know where we are."

He never says her name.

His voice is hard, the sounds harsh through his teeth, because of the way he forces the air from his mouth, and his voice continues when the movie is over.

We start the drive back, and I weave in and out of sleep, listen to him saying, "We need to get out of here," and Momma saying, "Where? There's nowhere for us to go."

Eight

Daddy's sister gives him money, and his steps are heavy when he comes back from the store. He steps sideways going up the stairs, slow, and I see why when I open the door. He's carrying a box. It's a new TV.

He nods for me to get out of the way. My sister jumps up and down when she sees it, her hands held clasped together, and creeps in close to watch him set it up, but Momma holds us both back. "It's Daddy's TV," she says.

The wires that connect everything together look small in his hands, and he sets the instructions aside as he sits on the floor, punches one button at a time on the remote until the TV comes on. It stays on, and he moves the recliner in front of it, flips through all the channels, then stays on one. The news.

The TV we rented in our old house was bigger, but the speakers are better on this one, because when Daddy turns up the volume as high as it will go, I can feel the sounds, and it makes me feel strange.

I look to Momma, and she's wincing. She says something, but I can't hear her, so she motions to me and my sister, then to the front door. We have to leave.

Momma takes us outside, and I can still hear Daddy's TV as we close the door behind us and step down the stairs.

We go to Daddy's sister's house. She's making cookies, her hands dusted with flour. She waves us in, and Momma sits at the table as my sister and I help Daddy's sister bake. We make ginger snaps, dough mashed together with brown sugar, cinnamon, and cloves, and she shows us how to form the dough into little balls.

Daddy's sister mentions the money, and Momma gets quiet. She traces the outlines on the tablecloth with her finger as Daddy's sister puts the cookies in the oven.

"He got a TV," says Momma.

Daddy's sister doesn't reply as she sets the timer on the oven.

"With your money," Momma says. "He got a new TV with it."

"I can give you more," she says.

"No," says Momma. "We've already taken so much. We can't take any more."

Momma's hands go to her face. "I just wish—" she starts.

Daddy's sister sits at the table with her. She takes Momma's hands from Momma's face. "Let him have the TV," she says. "Whatever makes him happy. It'll help him stay calm."

Daddy's sister pets Momma's hand.

"You want that," she says to Momma.

"I know."

The house gets warm with the oven on, and Daddy's sister sets the cookies on a plate, piles it high with each batch, and wraps it with plastic wrap. Before she does, we eat a cookie each, a taste test as Daddy's sister calls it, then she gives us a plate to take home, tells us to give it to Daddy.

Daddy's still watching the news, the volume still loud, when we go back to the room above the garage. It's dark now, and the only light is from the TV, casting shadows on everything as we change into our pajamas and get ready for bed. Momma kneels by the blankets on the floor and kisses my sister goodnight.

The ginger snaps are still warm, and I unwrap them where Momma set the plate on the counter.

I take the plate to Daddy.

The TV's light flickers over his face, and his skin looks pale in the light, the angles of his face harsher and more defined. He wears a short-sleeved shirt, and I see the rippled skin that stretches from behind his ear down his arm.

I asked him about it, years ago when he didn't take his shirt off when we went to the pool, and he was quiet, eyes ahead. I thought he didn't hear, then touched him, the skin that wasn't like mine, and he flinched, slapped me away.

I asked Momma when we were taking a bath, washing the chlorine from our hair, why Daddy was different, why his skin was strange and not like ours.

"Fire," she said. "He got burned when he was a little boy."

"Who?" I asked. "Who burned him?"

Momma pulled us out of the tub, patted us dry.

"Momma," I said. "Who?"

Her movements were slow.

"His momma was sick," she said. "She was a different person back then."

I wanted to touch it at that moment, to see what skin felt like after it had melted away and come together again. I wanted to ask him what he did, what anyone could do to be punished with fire, but I never did.

I'm afraid to touch Daddy now as I watch the TV's reflection on his skin.

"Daddy?"

He turns toward Momma, calls her, and I step back.

Momma comes, takes my shoulders in her hands, and puts the plate back on the counter. She leads me to bed.

I lie down next to my sister, and Momma prays with us, and when she kisses me good night, she follows my gaze, looks to Daddy, too.

"He's just tired," she says, patting my arm and when she gets up, I fall asleep to the sounds of the newscasters on the television, of the men in suits telling of a robbery at the 7-11 by the road leading down the mountains, of the guns the burglars used to get their money, and the sirens as they ran away.

Nine

Daddy's sister takes us on errands after she gets off from work, so that we can leave Daddy be, let him clear his mind. She collects us at the front door, but never comes inside, and when we leave, she's always the last person to go down the stairs. On Sunday, she collects us for church, stays behind again, and when I reach the bottom of the steps, I turn around and see that she's still at the front door, looking inside.

My sister sees, too, and calls for her, but Daddy's sister doesn't turn. Even with her back to me, I can see that she's talking. She's saying something to Daddy, but I don't know if Daddy answers back or if he hears her at all.

She turns and closes the door, and her lips tighten together, then she smiles when she sees us looking. I don't know if it's a good or a bad thing.

We stay out longer than we usually do. Daddy's sister takes us to the hardware store in the afternoon to buy wood, nails, and wire. She carries a drawing with her of a tall room, levels marked off in inches, blurred after being erased, redrawn many times, and shows it to the people who work at the store, and they add hinges, point her to the wood cutting station at the end of the aisle. The snow has begun to melt outside, and she wants to make a chicken coop.

They've had chickens before, my cousin tells me as we watch a man measure and saw the wood down to small boards. She tells me about the mornings they harvested the eggs, reaching in the coop when it was still dark, taking eggs that looked different from the white ones at the store, brown ones still warm and that smelled of hay. She gave the birds names, spoke to them as they woke, and I watch her hands as she describes how she used to lift them and move them to the side.

"The birds are coming next week," she signs to my sister. "You can help me name them."

We bring the wood and wire from the car to the backyard, and while Momma and Daddy's sister hammer it together, we think of names for the birds. My cousin writes them all on a sheet of paper, and when Daddy's sister tells us we're in the way, we go to my cousin's room and think of more names while the hammering goes on outside.

My sister and I take turns with the sheet, narrow down the names we like, and my cousin opens her top drawer, gets out a candy cigarette, holds it between her fingers like I had seen Daddy's momma do, and my sister gasps, asks if it's real.

She smiles, shakes her head. "It's candy," she says.

I had seen my cousin suck on them before, and she smiles, offers one to me. I remember the cigarettes Daddy's momma smoked and the way she held them, her hands stiff and held off to the side, different from the way my cousin holds the candy cigarette now, delicate in her fingers. It smells sweet, like gum, and she sucks on it, watches us put away the names of the birds.

"You want to see something?" she asks, and we get on her bed as she opens her closet and gets something from inside.

She digs past her dance dresses, the blue sparkly one that I love to touch when she lets me see her clothes, and she picks up a shopping bag, puts whatever is inside behind her back, then faces us.

"Can you guess what it is?"

She signs with a single hand, and my sister signs guesses, gestures that get bigger and bigger each time my cousin shakes her head. My cousin looks to me. "Do you know?"

I don't, and she pauses, then draws it out in a single motion, and we both gasp.

A bra.

But unlike ones we've seen in the laundry, ones that Momma wears. It's a colored bra, a blue one with white lace along the top edges of the cups and the sides of the straps.

We reach out to touch it, mouths open, and my cousin lets us crowd in to see.

Our voices low, we ask her where she got it, when, and how it felt, and she answers back. Kmart, yesterday, wonderful.

We both ask then. "Can we see it on?"

She smiles at the bra in her hands. "Sure."

She closes the door and steps to the other side of the room, turns around, and takes off her shirt. She wears a white bra now, and while my sister stares at the floor, I sneak glances of my cousin unhooking the clasp, taking it off, so that her back is bare, and the muscles and bones underneath move as she puts on the new one.

She turns around, hands on her hips, and we look, but stay where we are, hands clasped in front of us, afraid to touch.

"It's beautiful," I say.

My sister nods, shy now that my cousin has her shirt off and when Momma calls to us from downstairs, we all scramble around the room, my cousin jerking her shirt over her head, us getting out the bird names again, sitting on the floor, pretending we never saw anything.

My cousin opens her door, and we all go down the stairs, and for the rest of the day, my sister and I look at each other, smile, then look away, try not to stare at my cousin's shirt, the hints of blue underneath, the folds of lace against the fabric when she moves, try not to think of what is beneath our own shirts, the bare skin of girls.

Ten

The birds come on my sister's birthday. They arrive in cages, and need to be unloaded in the coop one by one. Daddy's sister shows us how to do this and their wings flutter as she puts her hands on them and nudges them inside. She lets us help, and we pick them up, guide them in, too.

They look smaller than we imagined them to be, and we ask Daddy's sister if they'll be okay by themselves in the coop. The snow is mostly gone, but the wind is still cold, and I think of the way their feathers felt, warm and beating where their hearts were.

Daddy sister laughs, and waves the question away, tells us to watch for our cousin. She'll be home from school soon.

My sister and I remember the names for the birds, and we kneel by the coop, point out which ones are which, but we don't have time to finish. The bus is here, and my cousin gets off, and we follow her into the house, to her room where she's putting her backpack in the closet and kicking off her shoes.

She's out of breath, but she signs to my sister. "Happy birthday."

My cousin makes the sign for how old my sister is, her hand facing out, her ring finger touching her thumb. My sister smiles, repeats the sign.

Seven.

Momma and Daddy's sister are cooking in the kitchen,

spaghetti and garlic bread, and as my cousin turns on her stereo, plays it loud, the smell of tomatoes, onions, and oregano drifts upstairs.

Her room is small, but she spins and steps to the music. She got the part of Dorothy in *The Wizard of Oz*, her school play, and I watched her practice the songs at her window with her eyes closed. My sister claps as my cousin dances, and my cousin pauses mid-dance, takes my sister's hand, and places it on the stereo, so that she can feel the rise and fall of the music.

My sister smiles as she closes her eyes and when she opens them, my cousins signs. "Like the music?" and my sister nods, hands unmoving from the notes that continue to vibrate from the speakers.

We watch my cousin practice, dance to songs about a rainbow, a yellow brick road, and home until Daddy's sister calls us downstairs and we eat, plates heaped with noodles, meat, and bread.

Daddy comes to dinner, but is quiet as he eats at the table with Momma and his sister. My sister and I go to the living room with our cousin, sit cross-legged as we breathe in the steam of the spaghetti, and eat it slowly to make it last. I am hungry, and I know my sister is, too, but we don't take seconds, because it's Daddy's sister's food. Except for today, Momma only lets us go to visit my cousin after they've had dinner and tells us not to take any food home.

They're on the front porch when we bring our plates to the kitchen, and as my cousin and sister join them outside, I steal a piece of bread in my fist and eat it in the bathroom.

36

When I go outside, Momma says we'll play a game. She has a piece of paper with words written on it like *candles*, *balloons*, and *string*.

"It's called a scavenger hunt," she says, and we each get a list. Momma says we'll go around the neighborhood to check off the items, but quickly, because we'll get a prize if we win.

She walks with us down the street, but my cousin goes alone. We check off things until dark, take in shoelaces, pencils, marbles, and brown paper bags. Sometimes, people give us similar things—instead of a birthday candle, a big, fat candle that smells of pine—and we take them, too.

When we come back, my cousin is already there, and when we put our collection on the porch, she sneaks her own things into my sister's pile, gives her the tea bags, ticket stubs from movies, and the unopened bars of soap we couldn't find. Momma counts all the things and says my sister is the winner, gives her a dollar, and my cousin smiles, but I don't tell her that I saw.

Momma splits up the marbles, pencils, and balloons among us, and we blow the balloons up as Momma puts our collected birthday candles on a yellow cake Daddy's sister made. We sing Happy Birthday, but my cousin signs the words, and Daddy sees. I glimpse the muscles moving on the side of his head, and I nudge my cousin to stop, but she doesn't. My sister blows at her candles.

"Don't," I whisper to her.

The candles go out. My cousin makes the sign for applause, both arms up, hands twisting back and forth in the air, but doesn't look to my sister. She looks at Daddy. Everyone cheers except for him.

Daddy stands, skids the chair against the wall behind him, and goes outside.

"What's the matter with him?" she asks me.

"He doesn't like us to sign," I say.

"Why?" She watches him on the front porch, leaning on the handrails. "It's not like he doesn't know what we're saying. He and Mom both know sign."

They did. I remembered the words his momma would sign to them shortly before she died, words slow through stiff fingers, but I never saw words come from Daddy's hands.

"Momma says it brings bad memories," I say.

I don't know what these memories are.

My cousin is quiet a moment. Her eyes move from Daddy's form on the front porch to me.

"What would happen if you signed anyway?" she asks. "What would he do?'"

I don't know what to say, but she doesn't ask again.

Momma and Daddy go back to the room above the garage, but Momma says we can stay. We play a game. Hide and Seek. In our room above the garage, there are not many places to hide, but in Daddy's sister's house, there are so many more. We hide in the bathtub, under beds, behind doors, in the laundry hamper, and wait for each other to reach twenty, then come to find us. We almost never find my cousin, who reveals later that she was in the dryer or outside, against the rules.

The only time they don't find me is when I go to the storage space under the stairs.

The storage door is cracked, and some light comes in, and while I'm trying to hide, I see a box with books Daddy's sister sent Momma and that she sent back from church. One is not marked and has a leather flap, a string holding it closed. I open it.

It's a diary, and the dates are from when Daddy's momma died. The writing is different from day to day, and I recognize Momma's loopy letters in cursive, the writing of Daddy's sister, letters so much like Daddy's sharp script—As and Os big, Ts crossed low—but with a curl at the ends of her Ys, something Daddy doesn't do.

They write of what Daddy's momma ate, how much she slept, and in the later pages when she sleeps all day, the entries get longer, Momma's full of scripture verses, Daddy's sister's of what she remembered when she was a child. Opaque bottles of perfume on the dresser, the dark eyeshadow and lipstick, the hat and gloves Daddy's momma would wear.

Her writing gets smaller and harder to read, and I inch closer to the light. I read of the lamp that remained on during the night as she stayed up, talking to no one, saying bad words she usually never said, cursing the men she claimed were breaking into her room.

"That is when we hid," Daddy's sister wrote. "That is when we waited until our mother came back."

I stay in the closet until the game is long over. I read of the belts she kept in her room, the zip ties latched double around their wrists and ankles as she tied them down to her bed, and the knives she laid out on the front porch after her husband left her, the blades washed and dried, set neatly by small black stones.

Eleven

I dream about those small black stones. They're on the porch where Daddy's sister said they were. It's the brown house with white trim with two windows near the front—a house I've only seen pictures of, but I know it's where Daddy grew up, a small one that isn't there anymore. I hear Daddy inside.

His voice isn't that of a child's, but sounds like it does now. There are no words, only breathing, and strange sounds.

I wake up.

Daddy's in the bathroom with a clothes hanger in his mouth. He pulls on it, and his hands are bloody. He makes the sounds again.

Momma is crying and stands beside him, puts a hand on his cheek and his head, but he bats her hand away, tells her she's hurting him more.

His teeth were hurting him, Momma said. That's why he didn't eat anything at my sister's birthday, why he left when Daddy's sister brought out the ice cream and began cutting the cake. I thought she was lying.

I watch Daddy pull, eyes closed, spit, pull again. Blood on him, the sink, the floor.

He spins around, pushes past Momma to the kitchen, pulls out the knife drawer, picks the long skinny one we use for meat, and saws with deep strokes, making the sounds again. He chokes then coughs, spits on the ground. The bloody stream clings to his chin then drips to his chest.

He saws again, and two teeth come free.

Closing his eyes, he hunches over the sink, holds one tooth in his hand, the broken half of another, and lifts them up to see.

I'm quiet as I go to Momma, and we clean up the mess on the floor. Momma moves to the bathroom, scrubbing the floor in there, too, then the sink, faucet, and bathroom mirror. Daddy's red fingerprints are everywhere.

Momma gives me paper towels and ice to give to Daddy.

He's on the floor now, spitting blood into a pot, and I hand everything over to him. He takes them, his fingers wet and warm as they touch mine.

He says something to me, but I don't understand. His voice is garbled by soggy red towels. His breath smells like wet pennies.

I remember Daddy's accident in the garage in the house we lived in before we came here, a saw missing the mark, cutting his thumb through. The skin and muscles were gone, but the bone was still there, I knew, because he showed me before he poured alcohol over it, bound it tight with ripped sheets Momma cut from the linen closet. I think of when he cut his head open, a wrench snapping loose when he fixed a pipe under the house after the landlord didn't answer his phone. A towel held to his head slowed the bleeding, and when blood still seeped through band-aids, a piece of duct tape held his skin together, leaving only a jagged scar when he pulled it off.

The mouth doesn't scar, I remember. It heals faster than

anywhere else on the body. Momma told me when I had fallen off the jungle gym, split my lip through. I wonder how long it will take for Daddy, for the bleeding to slow and the tissue to close.

She washes Daddy's teeth and sets them on the counter. I pick them up. They're chipped, black grooves on the side, but the teeth are large, flat, much bigger than mine. Momma whispers under her breath, then closes her eyes when she dries her hands. She's praying.

She goes to Daddy, empties his pot of blood in the sink, brings it back, and they lie together on the floor. He is propped up on one elbow, leaned over, and she mirrors him, except with a hand she brings to his head then down his arm where his burn scar is.

They look small like this, and I feel like I should look away.

Momma repeats the same motion until Daddy is still. She doesn't say anything as she does this, but moves her hand gently, so that it barely touches him, but does, and he doesn't push her back.

TWELVE

When Daddy's sister comes to the room above the garage to take us on another errand, Momma says no, we'll do our own things today.

Our room is dark, and the air smells of last night, Daddy's pot next to the bed where he's still sleeping. Daddy's sister knows about the teeth. Daddy told her earlier this morning when she brought by the leftover cake from my sister's birthday. The cake is still on the counter where she set it.

Daddy's sister looks to him now and talks low. "Make sure he cleans it," she says. "Check him, too. If he has a fever, that's bad."

She shifts her weight from one foot to the other, and for a moment, neither one of them say anything. I can tell she wants to come inside.

Momma motions for us to come to the door, and we do.

"We're going to the lake today," says Momma. "To let him rest."

Momma closes the door behind us, and we all walk down the stairs. Daddy's sister is the last to go down.

"I have some aspirin in the house," she says as she follows us to the car. "He needs something stronger, though. I can call a doctor to get something for him."

Momma puts a hand on Daddy's sister's arm. "We'll be okay," she says. "But thank you."

Momma has stopped taking the money Daddy's sister gives us, small bills in a white envelope each time she gets paid. Daddy takes the envelopes now. I know, because those days Daddy comes home with lottery tickets that he sticks on the refrigerator. He plays Powerball the most, and the drawing dates are always circled. The live drawings air after the evening news, and he watches the little white balls with numbers on them fly around in a machine until one by one, the winning ones are picked, numbers that are never ours.

He says we'll win one day. We'll buy everything we want, and we won't have to worry about anything.

But I know Momma worries now, because we don't have enough money for anything when we go to the store. Aspirin is expensive, and Momma counts the money we have left. It's almost enough.

We leave without having bought anything and go to the lake, and Momma spreads out one of our bed sheets down by the shore. Even though it's chilly, the sun is out, and we take off our jackets, lay together on the ground. Momma empties out her purse, and we count all the coins that have fallen to the bottom. Some are shiny and others are darker, their ridges worn, and Momma picks one out and hands it to me.

"That's the year you were born," she says, and tells me to keep it.

Momma's told me the story many times, a long labor that ended in the morning when the nurses wrapped me up and gave me to her.

I ask about her, what penny carries her year, if her story is the same as mine.

"I was late," she says. "I took a very long time to come. The doctors had to pull me out, because I wouldn't come on my own."

She pulls her hair back from the side of her head, and shows me where she had marks for the longest time, where the forceps bruised her head, and says Grandma, her momma, always kissed her there before she went to bed, long after the spots had healed.

We flip over on our backs, and Momma tells us more as we look up at the clouds, stories of the nights she watched the stars with her father before her parents divorced, how they memorized the constellations, and how she had wanted, more than everything, to fly to the moon.

We can't see the stars now—the sun is too bright—but Momma draws out the constellations she remembers with a blue pen. We don't have any paper, so she draws on the pages of the address book she keeps inside her purse, the stars small in the margins next to the names of people we know. She tells us stories her daddy used to tell her about the stars as she connects the dots to make Andromeda and Cassiopeia. We like the story about Perseus best, and I memorize the way Momma makes the constellation of the running man in the sky, his hand in a fist.

We pack up to go back home, but that night before we go to sleep, I draw it as Momma did, but on new paper, and bigger so my sister and I can see each star that makes him. We tell each other the parts of Momma's story that we remember, of the hero who saves Andromeda, rescues her from the monster of the sea.

Thirteen

I look for the stars on the backdrop when Momma takes us to watch my cousin in a dress rehearsal for *The Wizard of Oz*, but the painted sky is blank except for clouds and a rainbow beyond them. The canvas darkens at the edges, but not enough to see stars.

It's cold inside the auditorium, and Daddy's sister leads us to a row of metal benches. On the stage, there's a toy house and a white picket fence. The only play I have seen before is the Easter play at church, one that is the same each year, the pastor playing Jesus, the choir playing the disciples and townspeople, and the altar call at the end after Jesus rises from the dead.

Daddy's sister takes pictures during the show, and my favorite scenes are my cousin's, when she sings to the rainbow, when her house flies in the sky, when she makes friends with the lion, tin man, and scarecrow, and when she finally goes home. The show is beautiful, and my cousin remembers all her lines, does all the dances as she practiced in her room. When the witch forgets her line in one of the end scenes, my cousin whispers it to her, something no one else catches, but I know, because of the way her lips move.

At the end, we cheer, and she runs up to us, still in her makeup and costume, holding her little dog, the one her teacher brought every night for the show. She's hot, sweating from the stage lights, her face flushed as she beams at us. "You like it?"

Daddy's sister hugs her tight, congratulates her, her mouth near her hair, so that it is muffled, and we all do the same before my cousin goes backstage again. She talks fast on the way home, of the way the lighting was wrong at the beginning, the missed cues for the witch, and the way the dog wouldn't follow her in the tornado scene and that's why she had to pick him up and carry him throughout the rest of the play.

"We couldn't tell," says Daddy's sister. "It was perfect."

It's dark when we get home, and Momma and my sister go up to the room above the garage where I know Daddy's sitting in his chair. I carry my cousin's costume inside her house—it has a rip that needs to be sewn—and Momma tells me to come up after I set it down.

When I drape it over her bed, my cousin is still singing her songs, twirling as she takes my hand and soon, we're both dancing. I know the dance—I've seen her dance the number many times—but she is much better than me, her legs strong, graceful as she steps in tune with the music in her head. We dance the tin man's dance, arms hooked then not as we skip around each other, then side by side. It's one of her fastest dances, and when it is over, we are breathless and laughing.

She falls back on her bed, and I fall back, too, so that we're side by side.

"I wish you could have been there on stage," she says. "With me. You're good at this."

I wished, too. I knew everyone's lines and knew their dances.

"Everything changes when the lights come on," she says. "You don't even see the audience. It's like you're actually there."

We stare at the ceiling for a moment, then I close my eyes. I imagine myself there, too, and see the yellow brick road, the forest, and land of Oz beyond it. I see the sky and the rainbow my cousin sings of, the one that makes her sad in the song, because she cannot go there, and I become sad, too.

"I wish we could go there, for real," I say.

I still have my eyes closed, but I feel her take my hand. Her fingers are warm.

"I know," she says. "Me, too."

Fourteen

I sing my cousin's songs for days, and sign them, too, when Daddy's not looking, and my cousin teaches me the signs for words I don't know, words for wizard and rainbow. I teach the songs to my sister, and she copies the signs as we sing without moving our mouths, our hands swaying to music that is only ours.

Momma watches us on our way to church, and afterwards, tells me that she's volunteered to lead the outreach service. She says we'll create an Easter program, one that I can be in with other kids. "There'll be songs," she says. "Like the ones in the play we saw."

The songs are ones we don't sing or sign. Momma plays them on a stereo the church gives us, plays them loudly, so we can mime the stories behind them. The church gives us bed sheets to use as costumes, and we wear them over our clothes as we ride down the mountain to where the convalescent homes are.

My cousin plays John, the disciple Jesus loves, a man who asks Jesus who will betray him, and cares for his mother when Jesus dies. I play Peter who falls asleep in the Garden of Gethsemane, cuts off the Roman servant's ear when they take Jesus away, and falls to his knees when he hears the cock crow. My sister plays Jesus.

We go to a new hospital each week and as the nurses

wheel the patients into the lobby, we mime the Easter story as Momma sits by the stereo. My sister pretends to ride a donkey into Jerusalem, eat with her disciples, and pray in the garden. We watch Momma for cues, look to Jesus when we eat together for the last time, and cry when we see our Lord being whipped, tied to a post, on his head a crown of thorns. My sister plays like Momma taught her to do, pretends everything's real, that the cross is heavy, that the walk to Golgotha is long. When Jesus is crucified, she holds her hands out to the side, looks up to the sky, and gives her spirit to God.

It isn't like what my cousin said it would be. There is no stage or lights, and I see everyone in front of us. They are quiet, some not watching at all as they lie with their heads back, tubes in their throats. Some respond, hands clapping together, then upraised. One lady doesn't do anything, but watches us just the same.

She sits by the window, away from everyone else, and when the show is over, I take off my costume and go to her. Momma prays with the others and holds their hands. She has her Bible and holds it clasped in front of her, and leaves only after they've prayed. She stops next to those who can't speak, who aren't awake at all, but she never comes to us.

The lady takes my hand the way Momma takes those of others, doesn't let go, calls me child, and says things I don't understand.

Her words run together and she repeats them, but her eyes are sad as she looks to the other kids, to me, and I want to stay.

She asks my name, and Momma motions me to follow them

as everyone packs up and heads for the door. They go outside.

At the door, I stop and look at her. Her eyes are still on me. I bring up my right hand and wave goodbye, and she makes the same motion, her hand slow to come up, then staying there in the air until I leave.

On the ride home, Momma tells my sister and the other kids what to do next time, to face the audience more, to move around the stage, be happy, sad in certain scenes. I listen absently, watch the hospital get smaller and smaller behind us as we head back up the mountain, think of the way the lady by the window smelled of soap, her fingers on my hands, her skin fragile, thin like moth's wings.

Fifteen

The church gives us money for gas to drive down the mountain, but sometimes, they give us too much, and Momma buys groceries with the extra. The last Easter performance is farthest away, and after Momma fills up the gas tank, all the money's gone.

She counts the cans of food we have when we get home, opens and closes the cupboards, the refrigerator, and counts everything again. Her fingers tick off everything we have.

In the morning, her fingers move less, and at night, they don't move at all.

The cupboards are still open the next day, and Momma hurries us into our clothes and takes us outside. Daddy's still asleep, his head turned away from us, and I want to wake him up. I want him to see the stack of newspapers Momma has on the counter again with job openings circled, to see the cupboards open with nothing inside, but I follow Momma out the door.

We go to the bank, and Momma gets out an envelope from her purse, pulls out orange bills that look like wide checks, numbers printed in the corner like money. Savings bonds.

The bank isn't open yet, and we look out the window at the sun coming over the pine trees. I count the cars in the parking lot and spy the people in their uniforms walking to work at Kmart, the dry cleaners, and the video store.

When she sees someone inside the bank, turning the sign

from closed to open, Momma opens the car door and turns to us. "I need you to stay here," she says.

She sees my eyes on the papers she holds.

"I remember these," I say. "Grandma gave them to us for college."

She puts a hand on my face. "We'll get them back," she says. "We need them now."

She leaves, and my sister and I wait and watch cars pull in the drive-through and give money to the bank in cans that fly through tubes. One car has two kids wearing paper crowns from Burger King, and I remember Momma putting those on us once, the feeling of it around our heads, tight, pushing our hair close to our foreheads, so we couldn't see.

Momma's gone a long time.

When she gets back, she has money, and we go to the store and buy food. Momma's slow as she walks down the aisles, counts up the prices in her head, and we help her scan the shelves and pick out the least expensive things. We come home, put the things away, and Momma opens the windows, lets the cool air in as she scrubs the refrigerator, the floors, and soon, everything smells clean.

She takes the phone, sits down outside on the top of the steps, closes the door and when my sister and I play on the floor, make a fort with blankets, the card table and chairs, quietly, because Daddy's still sleeping, I can hear Momma outside through the windows. She's talking to Grandma, and she's sad.

I think of the way she lies in bed now, more now that Daddy's always sleeping, says she's praying, but I never see her mouth move.

Moving closer to the window, so that I can hear, I catch pieces of the months we've stayed here. My sister's birthday, my cousin's play, our church lessons, things I know, but then Momma says a word I don't expect. Baby.

SIXTEEN

I think of the sign for baby after Momma puts us to bed, how I would introduce Momma's baby if Daddy let us sign. The words for siblings are different, and I know the word for sister, a combination of the words *girl* and *same*. The sign for brother feels awkward in my hands as I make it beneath the blanket that covers me—my hand coming to my forehead first instead of down my cheek—the word for boy—then both hands coming together in front of me, fingers in fists except for my index fingers which are held out side by side—the word for same.

The sign fits my sister, our same light-colored hair that curls like Daddy's, freckled skin like Momma's, and the way we say our words, pausing over certain sounds.

I don't know this new sibling, if it will be a boy or girl, or how it will be the same or different from me.

Daddy's sister comes to the door, and Momma lets her in. She knows. I can tell by the way she looks at Momma, touching her more now, hands down her back and down her arms, her body careful as she hugs her.

It's dark, and Daddy's sister goes to the bed where he is sleeping. Momma stays by the door. Daddy's sister puts a hand on Daddy's head and wakes him up.

I think Daddy will be angry, but he's not as Daddy's sister leans in close to talk to him. She talks to him differently than Momma does, looks at him rather than to the ground, and repeats her questions when Daddy doesn't answer them.

I watch their mouths, because I can't hear them, and I'm surprised when Daddy's moves. He never answers Momma.

"No," he says.

Daddy's sister takes his hand, and he doesn't pull it away. She leans in closer and kisses him on the cheek, then again, closer to his mouth.

"Yes," she says. "You can."

I know Momma's watching, too, and I look to her, but she hasn't moved from the door.

Daddy's sister runs a hand through his hair, the way Daddy does to his own when he's stressed, but she does it more slowly, stopping when her hands reach the pillow, then does it again.

"When you're ready," she says. "We'll figure it out. We always do."

She kisses him again, and I feel strange watching them, jealous for Momma, because of the sameness she and Daddy share, the sameness Momma doesn't have.

Seventeen

Before Daddy's sister leaves, she takes Daddy's hand again, places something inside it, and I know it's money.

In the morning, the envelope is still in his hand, but he's sitting up, counting everything inside, then folding it up again. From my bed on the floor, I read his lips, so I can count the number of bills, too. It's more than she usually gives him.

He moves slowly this morning and eyes the room as the sun starts to peek in through the windows. His neck seems stiff and as if it hurts him, because he moves his upper body with it, and when he eyes me on the floor, his gaze holds. I hurry to close my eyes and pretend I'm still asleep.

"Good morning," he says.

I open my eyes again. He's smiling, and I take a deep breath.

"Hi," I say back.

He gets dressed, his movements slow as dries his hair from the shower, pulls on a new shirt and pants and laces his boots. He smells different—fresh and cool—and I recognize the cologne he keeps in the bathroom, one he only uses for special days like his birthday or his and Momma's anniversary.

"Today is a special day," he says.

"Why?" I ask. I wonder if there was something else in the envelope his sister gave him, if there was a note, or even an offer of a job where she worked.

"Because we're going to the maze," he says, his eyes getting bright. He draws out the last word then smiles.

It's a maze he and his sister used to go to at an amusement park down the mountain, a place along the highway where a maze was fenced-in with four towers in the middle—checkpoints they would have to check off as they went through. He makes an outline of the towers with his hands, tells us about the different colored flags that fly from the top of each one, and the other things there—a go cart track, miniature golf course, and arcade.

On the drive there, Daddy tells us to look out the windows and watch for the maze. He talks about the last time he and his sister went, how he beat the record, and how the workers wrote his name on a board along with his time. He talks with his hands, and they come off the wheel until the car drifts and he jerks it back, goes on with his story again. His voice is lighter, and he moves forward and back in his seat as he talks to us, tells us about the way the people couldn't believe his time, how they made the announcement over the loudspeakers, and how they all clapped after they wrote his name on the board.

We pass by gas stations, the new Costco store, and then, we see it, and Daddy pulls in. The place is just like he said, a maze walled-in with white fence planks, towers that look like tree houses inside, flags on the roofs. It's still early when we get there, and the golf course and the batting cages are empty, but we go inside, and the girl behind the desk gives us each a sheet of paper, the towers drawn on each one with a blank box next to it to mark off. She gives us pencils, too, and Daddy pays her, takes us to the maze.

Sitting at a picnic table with Momma, he motions for us to

start the maze, and we do. My sister goes in a different direction than I do, but sometimes, I think I can hear her when she's close, which isn't often, because the maze is long and soon, the sun is hot, and the dead ends more frequent. She's at the third tower before she calls to me, and I see her, face hot, hair wild, and she signs to me, tells me how to get there.

I never find the first tower, and when I lean down to the ground, look for my sister's sandaled feet, they are on the other side of the maze, far from me, turning, running, turning again. I search for her, no longer for the towers, and soon, I find a door, and it's where we started and my sister's already out, her sheet finished. The one in my hands is still blank, and Momma's holding my sister's paper, looks from it to the towers, at everything marked off.

On the way home, Daddy drives with the windows down, and Momma's asleep in the passenger seat. She has her elbow on the window, rests her head on her hand, and strands of her hair come loose from her ponytail, fly in the wind.

She's said nothing of the baby, and I wonder when she'll tell me, explain why she absently touches her stomach, lingers in the bathroom, turned sideways. She's quieter now, more than she was before, and I want to ask her if she's sad and why.

I don't remember the time when she was carrying my sister, but I imagine it was the same with her, with me, Momma spending the mornings outside, breathing slow in the morning, hands clasped, eyes looking to nowhere, thinking of nothing and everything.

Eighteen

It's getting dark when we head back up the mountain, and when we stop to get more gas for the van, Daddy counts the money we have left, and I count with him like I did this morning. We already spent half of what Daddy's sister gave us.

Daddy looks at us in the rearview mirror. His skin is flushed, but his eyes don't look angry, but a different kind of wild.

He raises his eyebrows when he catches me looking at him.

"You girls want to celebrate?"

Momma wakes up, and puts a hand on him. "They're tired. It's been a long day."

"How about," he says, his voice like an announcer on a game show, his words long and loud. "We go to the movies!"

My sister gasps, her hands held together, kneading one another as she looks from Momma to Daddy, then to Momma again.

Daddy's eyes are bright now, closing only when he reaches the last word, head leaning back as he holds the last word, hands raising up.

My sister screams, puts her own hands up, too.

"Baby," she says. "It's late."

Daddy's voice gets louder.

"And get popcorn," he says, looking to her, voice getting louder still. "And ice cream."

My sister echoes him now, her mouth big as she tries to

imitate the way he says everything.

Momma says nothing, but looks out her window, her hand rubbing her face before falling to her chest then staying there. She closes her eyes.

He folds the money up and puts the van in gear.

He did the same thing right before he lost his job at the house we lived in before, spent all our money in a celebration that went late into the night.

We go to the movie theater, the one in The Village, and Daddy buys the biggest tub of popcorn they have, finishes it before the previews are over, and sends us out to buy him more. He talks through the whole movie, faster as the movie goes along, and he makes big motions with his hands as he talks. People look, but no one tells him to leave.

When the movie's over, Daddy wants to see another one, and he takes Momma's purse, asks her how much she has, but she doesn't need to answer. He's found what's left of the savings bond money.

"What's this?"

"I had to cash them," she says. "I didn't know what else to do."

Daddy doesn't look at her as he spreads the money. It looks like more than it is, because the bills are small, but he lets out a breath, and it sounds strange coming from his mouth. He does it again.

He's laughing.

"Look at this," he says. "Look at this. This is great."

He's yelling now, and he spreads the bills in his hands, and some of them drop to the floor.

"Come on," he says, and he bolts for the door. Momma picks up the bills he left behind, and puts them in the purse he's given back to her, now empty.

She looks at us, but her eyes are sad.

"Go follow Daddy."

He's outside, and when he sees us, he points down the walkway where the ice cream and fudge shops are. We get a cone each, dipped in chocolate with sprinkles on top, and Daddy points out the stores that were there when he was a boy and which ones are new. He makes Momma hold his ice cream when he goes in the toy store, then comes out with stuffed animals and a box with a bubble machine inside. He gets a necklace for Momma in a store that's full of glass cases, small glittering things inside, and after he pays the man behind the counter, he takes the necklace out of its case, tells Momma to turn around, and clasps it around her throat.

He goes into the floral shop to get flowers for his sister, and the man behind the counter asks what he wants, and Daddy takes different flowers from each vase, then throws them all on the counter.

"All of them," he says, and he moves his hand to span the store. "Get me everything."

The man takes a long time to put the bouquet together, and we wait as Daddy goes through the aisles, picks more that he likes, and gives them to the man, too. The flowers smell strong, and the ice cream I've eaten is making me feel sick. I want to leave.

When the man announces that he's finished, Daddy takes the bouquet up. He can barely fit through the door as carries it outside.

The man says how much it is, and Momma gets flustered. "I don't," she says. "He has the money."

We call him back, and Daddy comes in, still holding the bouquet. The flowers obscure his face and bounce when he walks. The baby's breath tucked in-between the flowers are falling out.

"It's in my pocket," he says, and I get it out, and give it to Momma.

Momma opens it up and pays him. It's all the money left.

She shuffles through the lottery tickets he has stuffed in the pockets and the plastic cards he has in each slot inside. She gives the wallet back to Daddy.

On the way home, Momma tells us to thank Daddy, and we do. When we drive up, it's late, the houses on the street are dark, but Daddy opens up the back of the car, and gets out the bubble machine, takes it out of the box. Daddy's sister and my cousin inside are asleep, so we try to be quiet, but Daddy's laughing as he puts together a big bubble wand, one that has a string tied to the end that makes the bubbles bigger or smaller when he pulls it toward him, lets it go. He dips it in the liquid soap, pulls it out, runs with the wand in the air, the string let out then in, creating a bubble bigger than him, my sister, and me.

Daddy runs back and dips it in again.

"More?" he asks us, loud, but doesn't wait for an answer.

Momma sits down on Daddy's sister's porch. She's looking

down, her head in her hands. I want to join her, stroke my hand up and down her back the way she does when I'm upset, but I stay where I am. I want Daddy to be happy.

He calls me to him, and I turn away from Momma. He runs back and forth on the driveway, and we run with him. The bubbles look strange at night, lit a greenish-yellow from the streetlights before the bubbles pop and are gone. I watch the way they float, how they follow Daddy's hands, obey when he cuts them off and allows them to be. Sometimes, he makes a bubble with my sister and me inside, a large one low to the ground, and I see the walls shimmering around us, until it breaks, and we feel the droplets fall.

NINETEEN

Daddy's sister sets the bouquet on her dining room table, and it's so big that there isn't enough room to put down plates when they eat, so they eat in the living room. My sister and I eat with them and afterwards we go upstairs where my cousin has a project for school. My cousin says we can help her, so we hunch over a big white poster board on the floor, pictures, and pens laid out all around us.

She tells us it's a poster of her family heritage, a year-end project for school before summer, and she points out the family tree, the empty spaces next to everyone's names where she will put pictures of them. The one she has of herself is a new one, her hair pulled back, lips drawn in a closed smile, and she gives me others to sort through, to pick which one is best to use for the other names on the board.

I choose one of Daddy's sister laughing, her mouth open big, eyes scrunched closed. I look through others of a man I don't recognize. It's her father, someone Momma said I met once as a baby, but I don't remember him. His eyes and hair are dark, his beard covers his cheeks and his chin, and in all the pictures, he doesn't smile.

"Do you remember your daddy?"

She seems to expect the question as she looks to the picture I'm holding, at the man staring back at her, then back to the board. "No," she says.

She gives me piles of pictures of Daddy's momma, his daddy, and some I recognize, some I don't. I saw Daddy's daddy only a few times before he died. We used to visit him at his trailer where he lived with Daddy and his sister after the divorce, and my memory of him is fuzzy, of his white hair, wrinkled skin, and the smell of his thin brown cigarettes as he listened to the radio. I recognize more of the pictures of Daddy's momma and shuffle through ones of her blowing out candles at her birthday, holding my cousin on her lap as she read her stories, and standing in the kitchen—in the background, the jars of jelly beans I remember.

My cousin already has one picked out of Daddy, his face cut from the picture and when I pick it up, it's an older one, his face young, but the same, the same as his momma's, and I put their pictures side by side. Daddy's nose is more angular, but he has his momma's eyes, her mouth, and the same heavy brow. I think of the diary I found under the stairs and wonder what happened when she changed, if her eyes got big like Daddy's, if her lower jaw jutted out like his, if she became stronger when she beat her children, stronger than she ever was when she loved them.

Twenty

Momma's in the closet when my sister and I get home. She's going through papers we kept from the house we lived in before, and we sit next to her as Daddy watches TV. We help her organize everything into piles. Daddy knows what she's doing, and calls to her during the commercials. He tells Momma that the government gives people a lot of money and that he's heard of people using it for anything they wanted—fast food, convenience store items, even pizza delivered to the house.

Daddy's faces us when he talks to her, and my sister reads what he says. She leans over to Momma.

"But we have money," she says, and Momma shushes her.

"It's all gone," says Momma.

She gathers what she needs and puts it all in an envelope.

"That and the money she gives us," says Daddy, then he pauses and claps his hands together as he turns back to the TV. "We'll be rich."

She. Daddy's sister.

"We'll be set," he says. "We can get some property, build a house, live just like we want."

Momma sighs and leans against the wall, pulling her legs to her chest. Her eyes look the same as they did in the movie theater.

"She doesn't have any more?" I ask her.

"We can't take it," says Momma. "It's too much. We need to

make our own money."

I think of the food Daddy's sister keeps in her house now. They don't eat lasagna or spaghetti at dinner anymore, but sandwiches with bologna, and it makes me sad. My cousin never said anything.

Daddy stays home when we go, and Momma drives us down the mountain to a brick building near the highway, an American flag out front. She gathers her papers, and tells us to stay quiet as she takes us inside.

She takes a number from a red machine in the wall, and we sit on hard metal chairs. There are a lot of people who wait with us, who watch for their number to flash up on the screen telling them which booth to go to and which person to see. A movie is playing at the corner of the room on a TV mounted from the ceiling. It's playing *The Neverending Story*, a film we aren't allowed to see, but as Momma fills out paperwork on a clipboard, we sneak glances at the corner, at the flying luck dragon, the horse that drowns.

Across from us is a man with a boy and a girl. He holds the girl in his arms while the boy runs to the entrance doors, tries to open them, comes back, then tries again. He isn't tall enough the reach the handles, so he pushes against the glass, and opens it a little, but it's too heavy, and closes back each time. The man watches. He has tattoos of chains on his arms, the metal links shaded around his wrists tied together with a lock.

Our number comes, and Momma gets up, motions for us to follow, and we go past the booths where other people sit and talk to workers in front of computer screens. We walk down the hall, around a corner, and find the number that matches ours. Momma tells us to sit on the floor as she sits down in a chair, pulls out the papers.

The lady behind the computer screen brings out a calculator, looks at Momma's papers, and Momma talks about us, the baby that's coming, how she teaches us at home, and the lady nods, doesn't look up from the numbers on the calculator. She gets out a chart, numbers in columns, shows it to Momma, points with her pen to where we are, to where we need to be for them to help us, and Momma shakes her head, says that was before, that's not where we are now, but the lady says the same thing again.

We made too much. We can try again later.

Momma's quiet when the lady gives her back her papers, and when we go back through the waiting room, to our car outside, she gets in the driver's seat, closes the door, and sits still. We drive up the mountain, and it starts to rain, and Momma begins to sing one of the worship songs from church, one we always sing near the end of worship before the sermon begins, a slow song where we tell God that we exalt Him and that He's above everything.

She sings the chorus, a phrase that repeats over and over, and for a moment, I don't know why she sings when we've been turned away. When I see her round the turns, she closes her eyes as the road begins to straighten ahead. She does this more the closer we get to home, and every time she does, she doesn't see the things I see.

Twenty-one

We go to the park to tell Daddy that we didn't get the government money. He and Momma talk on the picnic bench, and I can only guess what they say as Momma nods, pats Daddy's arm, looks away, then to him again. Momma seems tired, and she looks the way she did on the porch when Daddy made the bubbles in the driveway, except her face isn't in her hands, but looking to Daddy.

My cousin is with us, and we play Hide and Seek on the playground. The moving bridge is the safe point, but I hide far away from it behind the tree overshadowing our car, under the slide, near the Tic-tac-toe board where we played with Grandma—all places where I am close enough to see Momma and Daddy. Daddy's hands are in fists on the table and his head is down, so I can't see his mouth. Momma says the same words with hers, over and over again. "We can't."

I know what she's saying we can't do. We can't ask Daddy's sister for more.

I don't see my cousin coming. She comes up behind me and tags me, but I don't respond. She looks to Momma and Daddy, too.

Daddy's standing up now. His hands are open and out at his sides as he starts to pace, his neck tensing, so that his head tilts a little to one side.

"What's wrong?" my cousin asks.

"Daddy's mad," I say.

Daddy leans forward, his whole body tense now, as he talks to Momma, and she puts her head in her hands.

"What did she do?" she asks.

Daddy puts his hand to his face, too, but not like Momma does. His motions are quicker, angrier, and he turns away from her, then spins around again, and slams his hand on the table.

Someone screams. But not Momma.

My sister is leaning over on the table. Her hands are on the table. Her eyes stare up at him.

She screams again. "Stop it," she yells, and Daddy steps back, eyes blinking, as his brow furrows. My breath catches in my chest.

I've never seen anyone yell at him.

I scramble off the playground to her, my cousin behind me.

"Stop it," she says, her words louder than they should be and running together the way they do when she is upset. She had been watching, reading what they were saying, too.

My body feels slow as I try to run to her.

"Stop," I say under my breath, but not to him. To her.

Momma shakes her head and reaches an arm toward her. She is pushing her away.

I reach my sister and grab hold of her shirt. I try to pull her back, but her body is rigid, her stance firm. She's angry.

I can't sign to her—she won't look at me, so I take her hand, hit it her palm with my own hand, straight and rigid. She knows the sign. Stop.

She looks to me then. "Why?"

I don't know what to tell her, and she looks back to Daddy. He glares at us, then turns toward Momma, his body hulking over, so that he towers over her small frame. "You let them disrespect—" and he stops, his tense hands coming up again, and he turns to the side and closes his eyes.

I put an arm around my sister's shoulders, so that I am hugging her from behind. I feel her heart beating against my hand. It's fast and loud, like mine.

"Please," I say. "Please, Daddy."

I don't know what I'm asking. I only wish that we can go back to the playground, back to how everything was before.

Daddy steps toward the parking lot. "Get in the car," he says to all of us.

Momma is the first to follow him, and nudges us all in front of her. We ride back home in silence.

Daddy looks at us in the rearview mirror, looks away, breathes hard, and although it's hot in the car, gooseflesh rushes up and down my arms. My cousin touches me, signs. "Why is he so angry?"

I sign back, small, so Daddy won't see. "I don't know."

But I do.

We pull in the driveway, and Daddy shuts off the car, and we all get out, walk to the stairs to the room above the garage. My cousin goes to her porch, and I feel her eyes watching us as we climb the stairs.

"They didn't do anything."

Her voice is hard, unlike anything I've heard from her before.

Daddy turns around, breath catching, and I climb the stairs faster.

"They did nothing wrong," she says, her voice controlled, and although I can't see her, I know how she's standing, hands on her hips, eyes at Daddy.

Daddy lurches down the stairs, and Momma calls after him. My cousin doesn't move.

"This is none of your business," he growls, and when I look, he's pointing at her, finger aimed toward her face. "You know nothing."

He pauses between each word, his voice low, and I go inside, don't watch her leave, don't watch Daddy come up the stairs again.

We know what's coming next. My sister and I wait at the end of the room, our backs to the walls and wait for him to pick who he'll punish first. My sister wrings her hands, steps from one foot to another, breathes through her nose as Daddy stops at the door, crosses to the bed and sits. He calls us over.

"Get in a line," he says, and we do. My sister's in front, and Daddy looks at the floor, then up at her.

It scares me when he's like this, when he tries to hold himself back, and I watch for the stillness, the clenching of his fists, the closing of the eyes before he breaks.

"Say it again," he says. "Say what you said at the park."

My sister starts to cry, backs up against me. I hold my hands up and feel her back against my skin. Her body shakes, and I want to take her, hide her, but I know I can't. There is nowhere in this room where we can hide.

"No, Daddy," she says. "I don't want to."

It's hard to understand her, because she's crying hard now as she draws herself in, hands to her chest.

"I said," he says, his voice hard. "Say it again."

I'm shaking now, and my sister takes another step back, straightens, and holds her breath, her chest still hitching. Her face is red, and she looks to him. Daddy's face hasn't changed, and the muscles of his forearms twitch, his fists grow tighter, so that parts of his hands are white.

She takes a breath, holds it again. "Stop it," she breathes, and he springs free.

In an instant, she's on the floor on her back, and Daddy's on top of her, holding her down. She's screaming, and Daddy puts a hand over her face, his hand covering her forehead, her nose, and her eyes, as he takes his other hand, puts it in her mouth. She chokes, and he brings her tongue out, and with the hand that held her face down, makes a fist, hits her chin, then again, and again until she closes her eyes, bites her tongue through.

Blood is everywhere now, on her, on him, the floor, and he turns to me.

I fall to the floor. He's on top of my chest, and I can't breathe. I feel his hand on my face, feel it brush past my lips, and I taste my sister's blood.

I can't see his face. Mine is covered by his hand, and I only see darkness.

I turn my head when he rams my jaw open, when he pulls my tongue past my teeth, turn it more when I know he will hit me, hit me as he did my sister, and it works. My back teeth

75

bite down, the ones I know won't cut as bad, and my tongue crunches between my teeth as my mouth fills, becomes hot as the blood comes.

I don't move when he gets up, don't look to my sister who is heaving on her hands and knees now, throwing up blood on the floor. She's crying between heaves, and Daddy kneels next to her. I can only see his feet and her lurching body.

I don't want to watch, but I do.

Daddy looks to Momma.

"If they ever disrespect me again," he says, and Momma nods and crawls to us.

He doesn't have to finish. Momma already knows.

We do, too.

Momma picks us up and takes us to the bathroom where she washes our clothes and holds ice to our mouths. She closes the door, but I can hear Daddy turn on the TV and watch the news stories, because he plays them loud.

My sister's stopped crying, and as Momma washes our faces, checks our mouths to see if they've stopped bleeding, my sister shows her where her tongue's been cut off, jagged where a piece is missing. Momma puts the ice back on, gives her a washcloth to put in her mouth, and we sit on the floor, wait for the bleeding to slow.

Momma pats our arms, holds my sister in her lap, and rocks as she hums one of the worship songs from church.

"Your daddy still loves you, baby," she says. Neither of us say we know.

My sister doesn't move as Momma continues to rock her,

and I get close to her face, and she looks. "I'm sorry," I sign. I don't care if Momma sees.

My sister furrows her eyebrows, tries to say something, but the ice, the bloody cloth are in the way. I sign again.

"I should have gone first."

Twenty-two

It's a week before Momma lets us out of the house again when our mouths have started to heal, and we go to the movies, so Daddy can clear his head. We drive to the drive-in theater, where we went when we first came here, and Momma reclines the seats, tells us to sleep again. It's a quiet movie, one about two people who fall in love, and I watch the reflections in the window, how the man brushes the woman's hair away from her face, kisses her forehead, and it makes me sad. I don't know what they say to each other—Daddy's talking too loud—but I imagine words sweet and soft.

My sister's awake, too, and we sign in the dark. She doesn't move her mouth the way she does sometimes when she signs, words difficult to say around a swollen tongue, spit that still tastes of blood. I know, because it's the same with me.

We sign about the stars, ones we see out the window. I like that the stars are brighter here on top of the mountain, not blanketed in smoke and fog as they were in the house we lived in before, and the constellations are easy to find. We look for the ones Momma drew for us by the lake, the ones she and her daddy used to find when she was a little girl. My sister finds the swan, the one that Momma calls the Northern Cross, and she points to the long neck in the sky, its wings as it flies over what we know is the Milky Way. We look for more, find the scorpion, and the eagle.

I find the lyre, an instrument Momma said Apollo gave to Orpheus, that he played for Hades to bring his wife back from the Underworld. The last one we find is Cepheus, the house that lies on its side, and I turn to Momma to show her, because it's one we've never seen. Daddy's still talking, and Momma's looking ahead, her eyes blank the way they are when she's sitting outside on the top of the stairs, and I stop, then turn back to the window.

The house only has a few stars, and my sister and I trace the house in the sky with our fingers, draw the floor, the roof, the walls, and it looks strong, even though it's toppled over on its side.

Twenty-three

There are stars on a letter my cousin writes me, one she leaves for me and my sister under our door after Momma doesn't let us play like she used to do. She draws hearts in the margins, too, and folds the letter up in so many ways with a piece left out that I pull and the whole letter comes free.

She writes of the chickens, which ones have laid the most eggs, and of the projects she's doing over the summer for school, the books she has to read, and the reports she's writing. She misses us, she writes, and she knows.

I write her a letter back, but on the back of hers, because we don't have paper, and my sister and I sign at night of what to say, the news stories on TV, the glass Momma dropped and broke when she was washing the dishes, the spider we found in the bathroom, details of our lives inside the room above the garage.

I fold it like she does, carefully keeping the creases where she folded her letter to us, and I leave it under our door, but at the corner where the hinges are, so if Momma or Daddy opens the door, they don't see it.

She leaves another one the next day. It's a shorter one, but instead of the stars and the hearts in the margins, she draws a telephone just like the one she has in her room, a pink one that's also clear, so someone could see all the workings inside. In the drawing, a line connects it from her room to outside her house through the city and to a building with the numbers 911 on top of it. *You don't have to talk to them*, she writes. *Hang up, and they'll trace it.*

My sister asks what it means, and I keep reading.

Do it next time it happens, and they'll know where you are.

Recorded calls are always on the news on Daddy's TV, voices frightened and broken up with other sounds in the background. The operator is always calm and asks questions, ones I know I couldn't answer, because I'd be too afraid to name everything they wanted. Our room. Daddy. Me.

I don't write her back, but keep her letter, opening and closing it when staring at the phone Momma has on the kitchen counter. It's not like my cousin's, but tan, and one that Momma can take outside.

I don't think the trace will work, but I wait until Daddy's gone. It's Daddy's sister's payday, and she's already come by this morning, talked to Daddy at the door. The lottery tickets on the fridge are old, and Daddy's gone to get new ones.

The phone feels cold in my hand when I pick it up, dial, then hang it up. I do it again, but hold the phone above the receiver after I dial it, wait for whoever is on the other side to answer, then hang it up again. I never put it up to my ear.

They never come, and I get her letter out again, write on the back, tell her it was a lie.

I am halfway through when Daddy's sister calls Momma, and Momma, still with the phone to her ear, turns to my sister and me.

"Who called them?"

I am afraid of who *them* are, but neither of us say anything. Momma knows it was me.

She charges toward me, takes me by the arm, and pulls me down the stairs. Momma's never touched me this way before, and I fight to keep up with her, my bare feet slipping on the stairs.

"Tell them you made a mistake," she says, and her voice quavers like it does when Daddy's angry. "Hurry before he comes back."

He. Daddy.

The squad car is in the driveway, and the policeman is still in the driver's seat. A German Shepherd is in the back, the window open, and it barks when it sees me. Momma nudges me close to the car, but far enough to be out of reach of the dog.

"Tell him," she says, but I can't. I am entranced by the uniform and the shiny badge on the front of his shirt. His arm hangs out of the window, and on it, I see little black hairs. He smiles at me, and while Momma talks to him, he doesn't look to her, but to me.

He tells me that I did a good thing, but to wait. Wait for an emergency. "Then," he says, "We'll come."

He waves to Momma, and I wave back. I like him.

Momma waits until he's gone. She pulls me back up the stairs. Daddy's sister is behind us. She's angry, too.

I go inside, Momma, too, and Daddy's sister pushes in behind us, looks behind her for Daddy, then to us again.

"What are you thinking?" she whispers, but she says it angrily, a yell-whisper. "What if he was here? What if it set him off?"

Momma tells her it was an accident, that we didn't mean to, and Daddy's sister turns away, hands coming up to her face, slow and tense, the way Daddy's do.

"We can't risk that," she says.

They are quiet for a moment, and Momma looks to us. "They won't come back," says Momma. "I'll watch them closer, it won't happen again."

Daddy's sister's voice is louder now, and she spits when she talks.

"We have to protect him," she says. "*You* have to protect him."

She looks behind her. Daddy's come back. Our van is in the driveway.

"When they took her away, it only hurt her," says Daddy's sister. Daddy's momma. The diary. There was only one entry that Daddy's sister wrote about *they* and *them*. Night, her mother naked, and scrawled words about fire I didn't understand.

"She got better after we got her back," she says. "But it took a long time."

Daddy starts to come up the stairs.

"If you love him," she says, "you will keep them away."

She eyes the phone on the counter, still off its cradle. She takes it up, and unhooks it from the wall.

She steps down the stairs, phone in her hand, and waves as she passes Daddy. She doesn't hide it, and he doesn't seem to see it as he walks past her and into our room above the garage. She doesn't turn back, and Daddy shuts the door.

Twenty-four

My letter is in pieces the next day. I pull it out of the trash and see parts of my writing, my cousin's drawing of the telephone behind it. It's ripped in uneven pieces, some smaller than others, and I know it was Momma. I put the pieces back and push them down to the bottom of the trash bin, so that no one else sees them.

Momma doesn't mention the letter, but then neither does my cousin when Momma sends us outside to play, so Daddy can rest. We spend hours in my cousin's room, and she's cleaning, so we go through her dresser drawers and the closet with her, stumble across her things, the candy cigarettes, the bra with lace along the sides. She gives us what she's going to throw away, a pair of white jeans, a blue skirt, and stickers left over from school projects the year before.

I put on the jeans, and they smell of her, a faint scent of cinnamon and the aloe vera she wears on her skin. I like the way they feel, and I walk around in them, try to stand the way she does, weight on one leg, hands on hips, but stop when she looks out the window, waves, then tells us to follow her down the stairs.

One of her friends from school is outside, and my cousin says we're going to her house, but we pause, look to our room above the garage, and she sees.

"It's okay," she lies. "Your mom said you could go."

The girl's house is across the street, the same one where we watch the cats sometimes when they are away, and we play in their backyard. They have a swing set and a slide that my sister goes down while my cousin and the girl sit on the swings, talk about the boys at school. I don't know the boys, ones my cousin says are lifeguards at the pool and who have a driver's license, take girls to movies at the drive-in theater.

I don't have anything to say, so I go inside, see the girl's little sister, and she asks me to play upstairs. She has a play house in her room, one with white walls, a green roof, a door that's red, and we play that we're neighbors, say hello as we go outside to check the mail and water our gardens. She asks me to tea, and we set the table, set out the pretend sugar and cream. I pour the tea for her from a pink teapot, pretend the tea's hot, and that we have to blow on it to cool.

One of their cats comes in. It's the calico, the smaller of the two, and he jumps on the dresser and watches us.

"He can't be in here," she says.

She shoos with her purse, but he steps to the side, jumps from the dresser to the table where the tea party is, spills the cups, the plates, the fake milk and cream.

The girl screams and goes after him, and when he darts under her bed, she stops, sighs, looks to me, and I watch her go to her door, shut it, then wriggle under the bed.

When she comes out, she has him. "He's been very bad," she says.

She pulls her pillow off the bed, takes off the case, wraps it over the cat, and holds him up. The pillow case looks strange with the cat inside, and then the cat moves and the pillow case writhes.

She hits the bag, and it moves more.

"He must be punished," she says.

She does it again and again, and when the cat yowls under her hand, she feels to where his head is, opens his mouth, and I can see the places where his teeth are beneath the sheet. She pushes into his mouth with her thumbs, and his movements become violent, claws finding their ways through the pillow case, and through all of it, the girl doesn't say a word.

Neither do I. I don't know what to say, where to look. I can only think of what Momma does, of what I remember of her against the wall as she watches, eyes on Daddy, on us, moving only when everything's stopped.

The girl puts the pillow case down, and the cat runs away. We don't continue the game, but leave the cups and plates where they lie on the floor. I go outside to where the others are and wait until we can all go home to the room above the garage.

The neighbors never ask us back, and I never tell anyone why.

Twenty-five

I see the clothes the neighbor girl wore at the tea party—a polka dotted green shirt and tight black pants—when we go to Kmart to get new clothes for my cousin after Daddy's sister gets a bonus. A child mannequin wears the outfit in the children's section, the head cut off, so that there is no face, and for a moment, I think it's the neighbor girl until I see that it's not.

Daddy's sister follows my cousin with a red cart as we all go through the aisles, pick out things that would look good on her, and she holds them up to herself, sets some things back, and keeps the rest. We go on our own to where the shirts are, and my cousin picks out some designs and asks us if we think they are pretty while Daddy's sister stays in the aisle with Momma where the baby clothes are.

Momma's looking at the newborn sizes, the yellows and greens, and Daddy's sister gets a blue one, holds it over Momma's belly, then trades it with a pink one, asks her if she's found a name. Momma hasn't talked about the baby much, and sometimes, I forget one is coming until she touches it, a movement where she traces the designs on her shirt, stopping when she feels the baby move.

My cousin taps my shoulder, and I turn to see her holding up two bras in different shades of pink, asking me which one she should choose, and I remember the first one she showed us in her room, the lace against her skin. I touch the ones she holds out in front of me, and the material is soft, the padding in the cups yielding to my touch. I pick the lighter one, and she agrees, goes to Daddy's sister's cart, and slips it in.

She goes on ahead to the shoes, picks out ones with heels, and I wait until everyone's ahead before I go to where Momma is. She's still by the baby clothes and picks up booties, baby caps that she looks at then puts back. The things smell different here, of powder and lotions, and I see her picking the bottles up, smelling them before putting those away, too. I look at the same things, and for a moment, I don't think Momma sees me. She's somewhere far away.

She pets stacks of bibs in different colors, and lets them go, then looks to where everyone else has gone and follows them to the shoes. We pass the bras, and I look at the ones my cousin was looking through. There are more pink ones, ones in red, blue, and green. Some are striped or have polka dots and the white ones in the corner are smaller and plain.

"How old do I have to be to wear one of those?"

She looks to where I point.

"You don't need to wear one of those," she says. "Jezebels wear them."

That's her word for women who have fallen from God, for the woman she pointed out to us last Sunday in church, the one who knelt at the altar while she prayed, who wept when the pastor put his hands on her before the congregation.

Momma had Jezebel's name highlighted in her Bible, underlined, then in her handwriting, repeated and circled in the margins, and I look to my cousin ahead of me. She's trying on new shoes, a white sandal on one foot, a brown one on the other, one with a higher heel, and she hobbles with the difference in height, then laughs when she trips and falls over.

My cousin doesn't look like what I had imagined a Jezebel to be, and I wonder if it's the shoes that make her a Jezebel or the clothes. Or the letter she had written, and the one I started to write back to her, if that made me a Jezebel, too.

We drive home, but I'm quiet as I look out the window, thinking only of the queen Momma told us of many times, who turned the king to worship false gods, who killed God's prophets, and who died in Jezreel, thrown from a window, then eaten by the dogs.

Twenty-six

Daddy's wallet is fat when he sets it on the counter. Some of the bills peek out from the sides, and they are bigger than the ones Daddy's sister usually gives him. It stays in its place as my sister and I wash the dishes, set them out to dry, carefully laying the plates and the cups around the money, so it's not disturbed.

Momma goes through her counting routine again with the cabinets and from watching her, I know that we have two cans left. She leaves the cabinets open. The refrigerator is also empty.

Daddy sleeps, and Momma waits until his head is turned away from us, then sets a hand on my arm, pulls me and my sister to the counter. She takes the wallet, slides the money out, and gives it to me.

She signs to us, and we both straighten, watch her hands closely.

"Give it back to her," she signs. "But hide it. Put it in a place where she won't find it for a while."

Her hands move slow, her fingers quiet as her voice would be as she signs the word for hide, a word where she moves a fist, thumb up and out, under her other hand, outstretched, palm down.

I look at the money in my hands. It's more than I've ever held, and the bills smell musty like they're old and have been used many times.

Momma hides Daddy's wallet in her shirt.

"Why are you hiding that?" my sister asks, and Momma puts a finger to her lips.

"He has to think he lost it," she signs. "Otherwise, he'll know."

She looks to the open cabinets. "He needs to know this, that we can't do this anymore."

Momma puts my hands over the money and pushes it toward me. I stuff it in my pocket and pull my shirt down over it.

"Go to their house," she signs, and she moves us toward the door. "Stay the night."

Her brows are furrowed, her face tight, and I know that she's afraid.

"Don't come back until Daddy's gone."

"Where are you going to be?" my sister asks.

I want Momma to come with us, but I know she can't.

She takes a deep breath as she looks at us. "I need to help him look," she says. "I need to help him believe that it's gone."

I don't want to leave Momma, but Momma opens the door and nods us out. I kiss her goodbye, and hold her hands with my own. I make the sign for I love you with my hands in her palm, and she smiles, does the same.

It's raining when we go outside and down the stairs to Daddy's sister's house. Daddy's sister is working, but my cousin is at home, and she lets us in.

We play a game, and my sister isn't shy about suggesting Hide and Seek again. We can sign freely now, and my sister signs that she'll be it, and she waves me away to hide. She smiles, eyes knowing.

I go to Daddy's sister's room, a place we never hide, but my sister doesn't look for me. The room looks smaller than I imagined it to be, and I wander around her bed, still unmade, look in her closet and her bathroom for a place where Daddy's sister will find the money, but not for a while.

I open her dresser drawers. Underwear and slips in the top. Pajamas second one down. Short-sleeved shirts and exercise pants in the third. I've never seen her exercise or run. The clothes are folded neatly. I lift the clothes up, feel around at the bottom. There is nothing hidden there, so I place the hidden thing of my own, the money, between her shirts, and I hear my cousin call herself safe at the safe point downstairs. I am quickly behind her.

Twenty-seven

I can't sleep that night. Rain continues to fall outside, but it's quiet as it builds. Smoke doesn't float from the neighbor's chimney, the dogs are quiet, and the light is on in the room above the garage. Daddy's still there.

The blinds are closed, but I don't see his shadow. I don't see anything, and I get up to put my hands against my cousin's window, feel the glass against my hands.

I miss Momma's hands and way she held my mine this morning. She always said I had her hands, had her index fingers that turned slightly inward toward my other fingers, the same swirls in our fingerprints.

I make my hands fists and draw them together toward my mouth the way Momma does when she prays hard. Momma usually says the words when we pray together at night, but tonight, my words are my own.

My breath fogs the glass and hides the light from me, so I stop, pray with my hands instead, something Momma never does.

My signs are the same as Momma's this morning. Daddy. Gone.

The word for Daddy is at my head, an open hand with the thumb hitting my forehead, but gone is there, too, and I pull the sign for Daddy away, pull it back into the word gone, a sign that pulls my fingers closed as it goes farther and farther away from me.

I lay down by the window, far enough away, so that I can still see the light from our room, and I fall asleep mid-prayer, my hand still closed in gone, a sign I prayed would stay the same, a word that would describe Daddy forever.

I'm cold when I wake up, and my sister's already gone, my cousin, too. I run to the window. I can't see the light.

Daddy's sister is eating breakfast at the table. She's in her bathrobe, and waves at me when she sees me. She hasn't found the money.

My sister's at the front window, and I see what she sees. Our van is gone.

Daddy is gone.

We don't wait to get dressed or put our shoes on. I pull her outside to the room above the garage.

The door is unlocked, and Momma is waiting for us. She cries when she sees us, and picks us up as she hugs us, and I feel her warmth against my skin. Broken dishes are scattered on the floor, the dresser drawers are out, and the bed stripped and tipped upside down, but we are happy as we help clean it up, make everything clean and new again.

I tell her where I hid it, and my sister tells Momma how she was the one who came up with the game, how she counted slow and didn't look for me, how she let me hide it where Daddy will never find it. Momma smiles and tells us to tell her again, and we do, loudly, because we don't have to be quiet anymore.

We eat from the last two cans in the cabinet, and Momma says Daddy will come back a new person, he'll look for a job, and we'll get a place of our own again. He always does, she says. "This will help him do that."

This. The empty cabinets. The empty refrigerator. The bare bathroom without toilet paper or soap. "This is what he needs to see."

We wait for him to come back, and the rain comes down harder outside. The wind picks up and the streets start to flood. Tree limbs fall, and the lights go out.

We get under blankets, and when night comes and Daddy still isn't here, Momma stares at the cabinets, opens, closes them, opens them again, fishes her hand in the back for anything she might have lost, but she doesn't find anything.

She tells us it's a good thing. She says we're fasting, a prayer God listens to more, something Jesus did for forty days when he was in the wilderness. "We are in the wilderness now," she says.

Twenty-eight

The rain keeps on all night and into the next day. Our candles burn down to nubs, and the room is full of shadows, but we sleep all day, woken only by Momma humming one of her worship songs. We don't get up for water—when we are asleep, we forget we're hungry.

We all lay together, and Momma's belly pushes against us. I put a hand out to touch it, and Momma takes my hand, places it closer to where the baby kicks under her skin. I feel the baby roll around and when it stops, she smiles, tells me I did that, too, when she carried me.

Momma traces my face with her fingers as I watch the baby move, and says the baby may look like me and my sister, have our same hands that's Momma's, the same hair that's Daddy's, and I pull my hand away.

"I don't want him to come back," I say, and her fingers pause on my face.

"Don't say that," she says, and brushes the hair from my eyes. "He'll be better."

Momma pulls the covers tighter around us, and pats my head. She falls back asleep.

I stay awake and watch the rain until it stops. The lights come back on, and Momma gets up to turn them back off. She tells me to go back asleep, but I get up, too, and look outside.

Our van is still gone, and only then do I get back in bed and close my eyes.

The room is warm again in the morning. Momma's awake, standing at the kitchen counter, looking out the windows. She's looking for Daddy.

Momma gives us mugs of water that we drink, and she gets in bed with us again, pulls the covers over us all so that it's dark, and we can't see anything.

The door bursts open then, and Daddy comes in, breathless, his coat wet, his face flushed. He's smiling, his eyebrows raised, and he lifts his hands, waits for us to greet him.

I turn over and hide under the covers and curl inside a ball, my hands in fists. They shake, because I am clenching them so hard. My face feels hot as anger wells inside me.

Momma gets up, then my sister, too.

No one asks him where he was. He answers us first.

"I did it," he says. "I sold the van."

"What?" says Momma.

Daddy puts a wallet on the counter, a new one, then takes something from his coat pocket.

"Pack your things," he says, then thrusts up his hand. He's holding tickets in the air.

They look like pieces of paper, brightly colored, with writing on them. Theme park tickets.

"Because we're going to Disneyland!"

TWENTY-NINE

It is a two hour drive away, and Daddy borrows his sister's car, leaves her a note taped to the front door. His scrawl is big, and he pokes through the paper with the pen. He doesn't sign his name.

The rain lessens the farther down we drive down the mountain, and when the reach the valley, the rain has completely stopped. When we get to the park, it's already crowded, but Daddy gets a map, points out the rides we will go on first. It's our first time here, but Daddy's been here before, knows which rides are best, and he takes us on them one after the other. The one with the longest line is his favorite, and we ride that one the most, following him as he pushes through the line, and we go on the ride with our eyes open, eyes closed, hands up, hands down, and make faces for the camera that flashes during the steepest drop. Momma waits for us at the end of each ride, looks at the faces we made in the pictures, and Daddy buys the ones he likes, puts them in key chains and frames, then gives them to Momma to hold.

Momma pulls them out for us as we sit down to have lunch, and we look at the faces we made in each one, and Daddy says the one in which his hands are out, mouth open, head back is his favorite. In it, he looks like he did the night we went to the movies and bought the biggest bouquet of flowers I had ever seen. His face is stretched in happiness, and I remember the way his voice sounded like an announcer's in that he drew out all his words, loud and long to last through all the applause.

"You made that same face last time," says Momma, looking at the picture again. She glances up at Daddy. "Remember?"

Daddy tells us of their senior year in high school, the day he surprised her when he picked her up for school, but then drove in the other direction. They skipped classes to come all the way out here.

It was raining, and some of the rides had closed down, says Momma, so people went home.

"Then the sun came out, and they opened everything up again," he says. "The place was all ours. We were at the front of the line for everything. We didn't have to wait at all."

Momma traces the outline of the picture, her fingers moving around each bend. They almost never tell stories together.

"It was a good day," says Daddy, and he gazes at her with a closed smile and when she looks up at him, he blinks at her with both eyes.

We finish our lunch, and Momma puts the pictures and key chains away again. Daddy sees a vendor he likes, rushes off, comes back with hats for everyone, and we wear them for the rest of the day. We go on his favorite ride again, and then go on the smaller rides, the flying swings, the swinging boat, and the spinning tea cups. Momma watches on these rides, too, and my sister and I hold on as Daddy spins the wheel, makes us spin faster than all the other cups around us. He's strong, and I try to follow his hands, but it makes me dizzy, and I look at what spins around us, the sky, the people, and the fence that keeps us inside.

Daddy stays in the cup when the ride is over, waits for it to start again, and we spin faster each time. The wind is cool, but Daddy sweats at the wheel, eyes straight ahead. At the end of each ride, he looks at us again, face stretched and beaming, eyebrows raised, asks us if we want more, and we always say yes, wait for him to turn the wheel once more, for the world to spin again.

He keeps going until the sun is gone, and we start the drive home. He talks about each ride, tells Momma as if she didn't see, and my sister chimes in, says which ones were best. He drives fast as he talks, passes the cars ahead of us, and I look at the drivers as we pass by. Some of them are alone, some with sleeping passengers, but I only see them for an instant, Daddy already pulling in ahead of them before the oncoming cars come too close. I look up, and the stars are blurred tonight, the clouds covering the constellations and the moon. The car quiets as Momma falls asleep, but Daddy's voice is still loud, saying things he's said before.

He stops talking when there are lights behind us, and soon we are on the side of the road, a police car behind us, Daddy breathing hard, moving his hand through his hair, his lower jaw starting to jut out. I pretend I'm asleep when the officer comes, asks Daddy questions, takes his driver's license, and after a few moments, the policeman gives Daddy a piece of paper, his license back, and lets us go.

There is no more talking from Daddy, only the breathing, the words he's holding back, tense in his muscles as he drives us up the mountain, faster than before, hugging each curve hard as we reach the top where the rain begins to fall again.

It's late when we get to Daddy's sister's house, and as Daddy pulls in, we see a car that's new, one that wasn't there before. Daddy leans forward to see, at what's inside, who the things belong to, and someone appears on the driveway, walks toward us. Daddy takes in a breath.

Grandma is waiting for us.

THIRTY

As soon as we get out, Daddy pulls the car back out of the driveway, and the wheels squeal when he pushes the gas, speeds down the street. I catch a glimpse of him, eyes ahead, face registering nothing, except for the pop of his jaw muscles as he grinds his teeth. I don't know where he's going.

Grandma rushes to us, her face worried, and she grabs at us like we hadn't seen her in years. "Where have you been? I call and call, but no one answers the phone."

Momma takes us inside and tells us to play while she and Grandma talk, but as Grandma walks through our room above the garage, we watch her open, close the refrigerator, the cabinets, and the drawers.

"Look at this," she says, pointing to the emptiness inside everything she opens, and Momma nods each time, says nothing.

Grandma looks in the bathroom, at our clothes washed and dried over the curtain rod, and touches the stiff fabric of our jeans and wrinkled shirts. She shakes her head, clicks her tongue as she had when opening and closing the cabinets in the kitchen. Leaning on the bathroom door frame, she looks at Momma, at us, and starts to cry.

My sister goes to her, wraps her arms around her, and I look to Momma before I follow, hug Grandma, too. Her skin is warm as she leans toward us, hugs us back, and I can smell the laundry soap on her clothes, one that smells of springtime.

She pats our hair for a moment, then wipes her eyes before she looks at Momma.

"How long have you been out of food?"

Momma doesn't answer, but looks outside at where Daddy had gone, and Grandma walks over to her, follows her gaze down the empty street. For a moment, they watch the rain, and Grandma puts a hand on Momma's back.

"Come on," says Grandma, and she turns around and starts gathering our things.

Momma watches her take clothes and shoes and put them in a pile in the middle of the room. "What are you doing?"

"You're coming with me," says Grandma. "You all are."

"He'll never go," says Momma, and I know she's talking about Daddy.

Grandma pauses, looks at her.

"He doesn't have to," she says.

Grandma goes to the bathroom, pulls the clothes off the shower rod, and adds them to the pile.

Momma doesn't stop her and soon, my sister and I join in. Grandma teaches us how to tie huge knapsacks—to lay a bed sheet out on the floor, pile our things in, then tie the corners together, so nothing comes loose. She makes it a game, and we see who can pack the most things, carry them across the room, and down the stairs to Grandma's car.

In an hour, the room is packed, and Grandma's car is full. The only things we leave are the dishes and Daddy's TV. The rest of the room is almost as it was before we moved in, the bed against the wall, neatly made, the card table and chairs folded and put away, the window blinds closed.

We wait for Daddy to come back and when he does, Grandma takes us to the car while Momma and Daddy talk in the front yard, Daddy still outside on the street, the chain link fence between them. Grandma has the windows rolled up, and I can't hear what they say, but I know that Daddy's angry, because he holds the fence tight, his hands in fists as he leans forward to talk to Momma, and Momma nods to everything he says, her hands flitting from her face, to her belly, then finally to her chest.

She says something to Daddy when she does this, words she repeats, and I watch her face to understand. She's crying, and her lips are hard to read, but she says it again. "For me," she says. "Do it for me."

Thirty-one

The ride north through the night to Grandma's house is long, longer still because Daddy isn't with us, and for hours, we drive down the mountain, through the desert, the city, and the fields beyond it, and then north to where the Redwoods are. Momma cries the whole way, but we don't talk about what happened when Momma touched Daddy's hand, and he flung it away, when he opened Grandma's car, heaved out all our things and threw everything across the yard, and when Grandma pulled Momma in, locked the doors, and sped away, how he ran behind us, called Momma bad words, then stopped and screamed at us all to go, because we—all of us—were dead to him.

I know Grandma wants to talk about it by how she looks to Momma, begins to say something, then catches her words when she sees us in the back. Instead, she points out things as she drives, the vineyards, the big bridge, and finally the cow farms as we get closer to her house. Horses graze alongside the road in pastures fenced in with barbed wire, and Grandma rolls down her window, sticks her head out, so that the wind whips through her hair, and makes the sound of a horse whinnying loud. The ones close to the road lift their heads, answer, and Grandma pulls her head back in, looks at us in the rearview mirror and laughs.

"I love doing that," she says.

She does it again when we pass a farm where foals nurse from their mothers, jump and run when they hear Grandma call to them, and Grandma points out the ones born last month, who came into the world in the middle of the day as Grandma watched from beyond the fence. She talks to me and my sister of them until we get to her house, tells us of their spindly legs, tiny hooves, and mouths she kissed when they nuzzled her hands.

Her neighbors have horses, too, and when we reach her driveway, she waves and says hello to them as she parks the car. Her house feels cool, the floors made of tile, and the furniture is large and draped with colored throws, the lamps on either side of the couches made with tinted glass. My sister and I roam the rooms that smell of leather and soap, and the bathrooms have dried flowers hung upside down on the walls, their stems tied together with string. On all our pillows is a small bar of pink soap, a washcloth to match. She knew she would bring us here.

Grandma and Momma come in, and Grandma shows us our rooms. My sister and I share a room where we each have a bed, the white comforters marked with pink flowers and green trim, a design that matches the curtains. Grandma's room is across the hallway and Momma's room next to hers, a crib already set up near her bed.

Momma cries when she sees it and touches the wooden frame and the soft baby blankets inside. The blankets are white, and Momma holds them to her face, breathes in, smiles, and tells us it's the baby smell, one we will know soon.

Grandma shows us the other things she bought, things she pulls out from under Momma's bed that she keeps in a laundry basket. Diapers, baby clothes with snap-on buttons, soap, and bottles. Some things we had seen Momma look at in stores, but others are new, and Grandma explains them to us, especially the ones she gives funny names to. The snot suckers are our favorite, and we laugh when she shows them to us, when she makes funny faces as she attempts to demonstrate, and Momma laughs, too.

Momma's laugh is quiet, a sound she makes with her lips closed as she breathes out through her nose, and I pause to listen. I missed it.

Momma laughs more when we go to the kitchen to make dinner, a feast of spaghetti, meatballs, and garlic bread. Grandma shows us the ice cream in the freezer, the root beer in old-fashioned glass bottles for the floats we will make after, and she gets out the whipped cream, sprays some in each of our mouths. It tastes sweet, and Grandma laughs loudly when she misses on purpose, sprays the cream on our noses and our chins, and for a brief time, I forget about Daddy and the mountains we left behind.

Thirty-two

There are no mountains here, and when Grandma takes us to town, it's a street with a post office, a feed store, and an insurance office. The storefronts look old, and Grandma parks her car at the end of the street and shows us the big rings anchored outside each store, where the old cowboys used to tie up their horses.

We go into each store, and Grandma introduces us to her friends, calls us her babies that have come to live with her, and they hug us like they've known us for years. They say they've been waiting for us and that Grandma's been hoping for this for a long time.

The screen shop Grandma owns is farther away, and we drive to the city where she parks next to a lawnmower repair shop and waves to the men who work there, introduce us to them, and they seem to know us, too.

We stay with her all day, and she shows us how she makes the frames, cuts them down to size, then lays the screens out and secures them down. She has rows and rows of screwdrivers, nails, and tools that we've never seen. During breaks, she shows us the rollers, the hammers, the pointy instruments, and big scissors she uses to cut rubber string. We help her find the tools she needs, hold them for her when she's not using them, and when she's done, she gives us each a penny and shows us how to fasten it in a vice, then lets us take a hammer, bend the penny over to its side, before she takes it out and gives it to us to keep.

The customers come in the afternoon, and we sit behind the counter by the cash register when they pick up their screens, drop off orders for more. Grandma knows them by name and tells us stories about each one when they leave, which ones had dogs, pools in their backyard when she went to measure their old screens.

When the shop isn't busy, Grandma talks to Momma about what she'll make for dinner, the friends she'll introduce us to tomorrow, and the people after that.

"Your friends seem to think we're staying here a long time," says Momma. "Like we're moving in forever."

Grandma gets out a yellow notebook pad she keeps by the cash register and makes stick figure drawings on it for my sister and me.

"They're just excited," says Grandma. "Like I am." She stops drawing for a moment. "And forever wouldn't be such a bad thing."

She draws the stick figures on the corner of the yellow paper, the figures moving a little on each page, then she flips through, and the whole thing comes alive. She draws some figures jumping, kicking, flipping over in the air, then adds more details, a mountain they both fall down, flipping over and over, before they land at the bottom and stand up again.

Thirty-three

We talk about forever when Grandma gets her calendar for the new year and sits at the table with all of us, writes down our birthdays and the days she'll take us to the lake when it's warm enough, to the old gold mining towns, and the forest where the trees are taller than anywhere else in the world. She circles Christmas and tells us we'll get a real tree today, one that will make the house smell like pine, like the mountains where we were.

Grandma skips forward and asks Momma when the baby will be here, and Momma makes up a day, one that is new to me and my sister. She never went to the doctor, said it was too much money, and we needed money for other things, but I pretend not to remember. The day Grandma circles isn't far away.

Momma makes marks, too, on Grandma's old calendar that has what's left of the year, small ticks on days she calls Daddy's sister when Grandma checks the mail or works in the garage. Momma uses the telephone in Grandma's room and tells me to keep watch. But she is never in there long—no one answers, and when someone does, they hang up when Momma says who she is.

The last mark she makes is on Christmas Day. We sleep in, and Grandma makes hash browns and bacon, and shows us new presents under the tree. A book of Bible stories from Momma, and from Grandma, new pajamas for all of us. Momma has presents for Daddy under the tree, too, but we leave those there. They're smaller than ours, and I wonder what they are, and if he has a tree, too.

Momma leaves when we make cookies with Grandma in the kitchen, and I know she's using the phone in Grandma's room. I go to the room, but I don't hear her talking, only stifled cries. She sniffs and wipes her eyes when she sees me.

"Daddy says Merry Christmas, baby," she says, and she wraps me in a hug. I feel her breath still hitching, and I hold her tighter, as tight as I can around her belly. "He says he loves you guys."

Momma doesn't say the same thing to my sister. She doesn't say anything about Daddy as she comes out and spends the rest of the day with us by the Christmas tree, and that is when I know that Daddy never said anything, and that everything Momma told me was a lie.

Thirty-four

We take down the Christmas tree on the day that Momma has the baby. Momma sits on the couch and counts between each contraction as we wrap up the lights and ornaments, and when the number Momma counts up to gets lower, Grandma says it's time to go, and we all get in the car.

The hospital smells strange, and Grandma takes us through hallways that are long, ones that all look the same until we reach the double-doors that lead to Labor and Delivery. The nurses take Momma away, and say we can't stay, pointing to my sister and me.

Grandma takes us home, and we finish putting all the Christmas decorations away. One of the ornaments is a cradle with Momma's birth year, and I ask Grandma how it was when she brought Momma into the world, what is was going to be like for Momma today.

"It took a long time," she says. "And she had the most pitiful cry when they took her out. There were two marks on the side of her head where they had to use these puller-things, and they took the longest time to go away."

I remember Momma's story.

"And you used to kiss her there every night," I said. "When she was a little girl."

"Yes," she says, and she turns to me, eyes blinking. "How'd you know that?"

"She told me," I say.

She smiles. "I can't believe she remembered that."

She pulls me close, and kisses me, too, and we put the cradle ornament away with the other Christmas things.

We make dinner, get in our pajamas, and Grandma says we can stay up until the baby is born. She puts on a movie she likes, one we haven't seen, of people who sing and dance in the rain. She sings along with the movie, and when that one is over, she puts on one about a carousel, how a man comes down from heaven after he dies, sees his daughter dance on the beach, but we don't finish this one. We fall asleep.

The phone rings in the morning, and Grandma wakes us up, tells us things as Momma tells her over the phone. The baby is here, a boy, and something is wrong.

THIRTY-FIVE

At the hospital, we go down the same hallways and double-doors as we did before. We stop at a nurse's station, and the lady behind the desk points to the room where they have Momma. We go in, and Momma's in bed, and the baby is next to her, on his back in a crib on wheels.

He's awake, but I'm afraid to touch him, his body so small, hands and fingernails that look miniature next to mine. There is a thin coating of hair on his head, and I reach in to touch it, and it feels soft, almost downy, and I motion for my sister to do the same, and she does. She is even more careful than me, and pulls her hand back anytime he moves, wringing them in front of her like she does when she's nervous. She laughs, then tries again, and we both touch his head now, our fingers touching as we stroke his hair. He stirs, and she doesn't pull back, but looks at me, smiles, then looks to him again.

Momma watches us and puts her hands over ours, pats him with us, on his head, his arms, his belly, and I watch the baby's eyes as we do, but he doesn't seem to see us, his eyes elsewhere.

The nurse comes in and has a clipboard. For a few moments, the room is quiet as the lady checks the baby's skin and his eyes, then writes things down. Grandma asks questions, and the nurse points out things on the baby, his pale skin, his eyes that don't respond, and the reflexes that aren't there. She snaps her fingers around the baby's head and when he doesn't turn, the nurse says a word we all know. Deafness.

Grandma clicks her tongue the way she did when looking through our empty cabinet at home. The nurse points to the baby, and Grandma makes the noise again, shakes her head, and twists her mouth the way she does when she trying not to cry. She looks at Momma, but Momma is looking away.

"We need to do tests," says the nurse, and she lists everything on her clipboard—genetic diseases, a stroke in the womb, not enough oxygen during development, brain damage—different things the doctors are looking for, and Momma interrupts her, her voice loud.

"No," she says, and the nurse tells her the things listed on the clipboard again, but Momma cuts her off. "No, I don't want to know."

Thirty-six

The baby is different than what Momma told me he'd be like when we finally bring him home. He doesn't take the bottle and cries a lot when Momma holds him, walks him up and down the hallway at night. She told me that the baby would look at me if I held him, that his tiny fingers would grasp mine, and it would be the best feeling in the world, but he never does any of these things.

Momma goes into Grandma's room as she did before when she called Daddy's sister, but her hand just rests on the phone now and doesn't pick it up.

She writes a letter, and I watch my brother when she writes, the letter long and full of crossed out things. She talks under her breath when she does this, and her face gets closer and closer to the page as she starts to cry again. Grandma finds us when Momma rips up the letter and starts again.

"I need to talk to him," she says, and Grandma pulls Momma to her until Momma's head is beneath her chin, and she pats her hair the way Momma does to mine after I've had a bad dream.

"He needs to see his son," she says.

Grandma pats Momma's head more and purses her lips as she breathes out slowly the way she does when she's holding her words in.

"I miss him," Momma says.

She works on the letter again at night, and I stay up to watch her pace the hallway as she recites what she wants to say. She sees me and tries to smile as she motions me over, and although I can't hug her the way Grandma does, I try anyway, wrapping my arms around her, my head against her body, now soft, and she puts a hand on my head, sets the letter down.

She lets me stay up with her, and I help her get the diapers, the baby clothes, and the rags she needs. She shows me how to hold the baby, feed him, and swaddle him tight, and teaches me little tricks that will quiet him—patting his back, his belly, bringing my mouth close to him when I talk to him, so that he can feel my breath on his skin, and I smell the baby smell Momma loves, of milk, powder, and something else I can't name.

It gets later, and I sit on the floor and close my eyes. Momma thinks I've fallen asleep, and as she paces the room, rocking my brother, she talks quietly like she does when she prays.

She's talking to Daddy, except not, the letter still on the table.

I open my eyes. She's looking out the window.

She tells Daddy she's sorry and asks him to forgive her, and it sounds like the prayer Momma makes us say when we've done something wrong, and we must ask God to make us clean again. She calls it the sinner's prayer.

She prays to Daddy again.

"Please," she says. "I'll never leave you again."

Thirty-seven

Momma's letter comes back unopened, stamps across the front with a sharp script next to Daddy's name. Return to sender.

It's the same writing from the diary I found under the stairs at Daddy's sister's house, the *T*s crossed low, the letters sharp and written with a heavy hand. Her writing hasn't changed.

Grandma sees it before Momma does and leaves it out on the counter, so that she can see, but Momma doesn't pick it up, and it stays there even after Momma sits down to write another and another after that.

She takes us to our room when Momma writes, so we don't see her cry, and she plays with us, helps us drape our comforter over the gap between our beds, so we live in a cave, similar to what we did in our old house, and Grandma teaches us tricks for how to make it stronger and to keep the blanket from falling down.

Before we go to bed, she reads to us. We give her the new book Momma got us for Christmas, an illustrated book of women from the Bible, and we leaf through. We start with Eve, work our way up to Leah and Rachel, then Ruth and Naomi. We spend most of our time on Sarah, Hannah, and Elisabeth, the women of longsuffering, who give up their sons to God, women Momma told us about, the son brought as a sacrifice on Mount Moriah, the son left at the temple in Shiloh, and the son who lived his life for God, who lost his head at the command of a king.

There are pictures of each one, brightly colored illustrations of women in long robes who look up to God, a bright light in the sky. Some of the women are nameless, the widow, the Samaritan, the woman who continued to bleed, and their pictures are different. They kneel, and the picture that I often go back to is the adulterer the men brought to Jesus to be stoned. The illustration is a close-up of her face near the ground, inches from the feet of Jesus. Her robes are ripped, her hair unkempt. She looks up to God as the others do.

We get to pages that are stuck together, and Grandma looks closer to see. These chapters are stapled closed. She pulls at them and bends the staples back, and the chapters come free, ones of different women who are drawn standing, their heads high, their arms upraised. In Deborah's hands is a staff as she leads her army to Mount Tabor on the plain of Esdraelon, a staff much like the ones we had seen men like Moses and Gideon carry in other picture books. Rahab stands alone in a tower after the city of Jericho falls, in her hands, the scarlet cloth that hung from her window that protected her when her city fell. The most beautiful woman is Jael who stands over the fallen body of Sisera, in one hand a half-empty bowl of milk, in the other, a bloody stake that she had driven through the commander's head.

After she reads these stories to us, Grandma fingers the places where the staples were. "Why would she do this?" she asks. "These are good stories, too."

My sister points to the blood on the stake. "Maybe it's the blood," she says. "Maybe she thought it would scare us."

But I remember the picture for Mary, the mother of God, a story Momma didn't staple closed, and recall the illustration of her next to the cross, on it, the crucified body of her son. There was blood in that picture, too.

We keep the book open after Grandma kisses us goodnight and turn the pages again. We play a game, Which One Am I?, in which we point to which woman we want to be with each turn of the page. My sister chooses the women she knows, Martha who prepares the house when Jesus is her guest and Dorcas who makes garments for the poor.

I choose women in the chapters Momma stapled closed and that Grandma opened up again. The women are bigger in these pages, drawn with their eyes open, their bodies and hands strong, their mouths formed in a prayer or a war cry.

The last woman I choose is Esther. She stands in the foreground of the illustration, her crown and robes the brightest colors in the picture. Behind her is her husband, a king seated on his throne. Esther's mouth is open, too, and in her hands is the decree written for the extinction of herself, her people, and her cousin who refused to bow down, a decree Grandma read to us that she destroyed, its writer then hanged from gallows 75 feet high.

Thirty-eight

My sister and I dress up like the Bible characters we like. We bring the book to the garage where Grandma has a chest full of old clothes and fabrics. Wearing dresses that are too big for us, we drape sashes over our heads and around our bodies until we, too, look like old Bible women from the past.

Grandma cuts off the hems of the dresses, so we don't step on them. She plays along, is the man we need in our games, plays the kings, prophets, and God, her voice low, her face stern as she walks around, her movements stiff, and we laugh, because she's not like the characters in Momma's stories.

The games stop when Momma's hospital bills come in the mail, and Grandma gets another job as a clown for children's parties on the weekends. It's a job she used to have when Momma was a little girl, and Grandma shows us where she keeps her costume, a uniform with polka dots on one side, stripes on the other that she wears with a green wig and huge red shoes. She puts her make-up on in the mornings before she goes and when the house is still quiet, she sits me in front of the mirror with her, shows me how to make her face white with a small sponge, to draw big arching eyebrows and lips that extend far beyond her own. She puts on a foam nose, slides on big gloves, and stands in front of the mirror, blinks a few times, and becomes someone new.

She doesn't talk when she's in her costume, and I have to

read what she wants to say in her face, her gloved hands that come out in front of her, and her legs that hop around in her huge red shoes.

I help her load her props into the car—multi-colored balloons, hats, and an umbrella—and when she leaves, I wait all day for her to come back, wash the make-up off, and give me her costume to fold up and put away until she goes out again.

I go with her once. It's my birthday, and I'm turning eleven, and Grandma says to pretend it's my own party we're going to and that the kids there are my friends. The party's at an empty warehouse with blow-up playgrounds with mesh walls inside, inflatables Grandma calls "bouncy castles," and as Grandma blows up balloons, makes them into animals for the kids, I jump in the bouncy castles until it's time to sing.

The birthday girl is young, younger than my sister, and she smiles as Grandma covers the girl's eyes until the cake with sparkling candles is in front of her, then uncovers them when all is ready, and the song begins. Grandma dances around everyone as they wish the girl a happy birthday and claps her hands as the girl blows out the candles. Grandma kneels down by the girl as people take pictures. She smiles between flashes, then hugs the girl close so their faces are almost touching.

The girl opens the presents that her parents lay out in front of her, and she screams when she tears the wrapping paper off to find plastic cooking sets and doll houses. While the parents gather around, kneel and take more pictures, I watch the other kids take off their party hats and play in the bouncy castles again. Two of them play a game I know.

They take turns in the inflatables as one counts and the other hides. There are many spots to hide here, and I remember when my cousin played this game with us in the mountains. I follow them, take note of where they go, keeping far enough behind them, so they don't see me and know what I am doing.

The game starts again, and I wait a moment then follow the one whose turn it is to hide, but stop when I get inside. The kid is gone, but a man is looking at me from outside the mesh wall.

He has a camera in front of his face, but he's tall, has wide shoulders and thick forearms covered in light-colored hair. The camera lowers, and I see his eyes, eyes like Daddy's, and I don't move.

A chill runs up my body. I can't breathe.

But it isn't Daddy. The man has a moustache, one that Daddy doesn't have.

And Daddy isn't here.

Thirty-nine

On the weekends after that, we clean houses while Grandma is at her birthday parties. Grandma helps us make flyers, and we pass them out in the neighborhood, and some of Grandma's friends are our first customers. We give them discounts if they have us come back more than once, and they live close enough for us to walk to and come back without using Grandma's car. We always come back before she does, and we set the money we've earned on the kitchen counter, small folded bills that Grandma will see.

The person who pays us the most is a lady who lives at the house at the end of the street. It's a big house with lots of rooms and always takes us longer because of the laundry we clean there, too, and the dishes she pays us to do. Sometimes, she gives us a list of extra chores—clean the wooden shed in the back, beat out the rugs, run a cycle of bleach through the laundry. The lady is a collector of porcelain dogs, a multitude of small, smooth creatures that litter the top of the TV, the windowsills in every room, and shelves above her bed. Some of them, she gives names to, the inscriptions written in black on their bellies when I pick them up to dust underneath. My sister and I think of names for the others, and she helps me with the ones on the windowsills, making sure each dog is put back where it was before.

The house is the only one I've seen where the vacuum

connects to the house, a huge hose I help Momma connect to the wall, and I watch her clean the rugs, my brother asleep in a sling around her chest. We move from room to room, and Momma gets out attachments she uses on the couch and the drapes, and when everything's almost done, we clean the spare room where all the paintings are.

Her husband sits in there, an old man with an oxygen tube under his nose, and he's always in a blue bathrobe, his feet in socks, and the lady always tells us to be sure the drapes are opened for him so he can see outside. He has Alzheimer's, she told us the first time we came and Momma explained that it's when a person forgets things, and we tell him who we are each time we come in. Sometimes, he knows us and waves, but most of the time, he's asleep, and we dust the paintings, clean up the tissues he's dropped on the floor, and pull open the shades.

He used to be an artist, an art teacher at the local college, and the paintings are his—dozens of them stacked one against the other on the floor against each wall. The paintings are all of people—children, mostly. Some of them are unfinished—a little boy sitting on the beach, his hands in the sand, two girls in a field, running, their dresses flowing behind them, and in the back, a man who walks alongside a little girl holding a yellow balloon. They are walking away, their backs facing me, and I can tell that it's summer from the clothes they wear. They are holding hands, the girl looking up at him, happy, the colors bright on her face, but the man's face is one I can't see, looking down and hidden in a shadow.

On the day Momma lets me dust in this room alone, the

man sees me looking at the picture and points.

"Little girl," he says, and he points again. "Little girl, little girl."

I don't know if he is talking to me or telling me about the little girl in the painting. I nod to him, and dust that one, too, then put the paintings I like in front of it, a barn with a door hanging ajar, and one of the yellow balloon the little girl was holding in the other picture, except the balloon is the only thing in the painting, untethered and floating away in the sky.

Forty

Four months after we move to Grandma's is the day Daddy calls.

It's late when he does, and I'm asleep, but Momma wakes me, tells me to hold my brother while she takes the call. I take him and follow her out to the living room, but Momma goes outside and shuts the door behind her.

I feed him, and try to rock him the way Momma does, but he cries, his voice raspy from the crying he's done all day. Momma seems to be gone a long time. I look for Grandma.

She's in her room, but sitting on the floor next to her bed. She's on the phone, too, but her hand is over the receiver. She hangs her head and closes her eyes.

She's listening to Momma, something I didn't know she could do.

I want to listen, too, but Grandma looks at me when my brother's crying gets louder, and quietly hangs up the phone. Momma is still talking outside.

Grandma takes my brother from my arms and walks me back to bed.

He quiets as she places the covers over me, and she kneels down, smoothes back my hair.

"Is Daddy coming here?" I ask.

Her face changes as she tightens her lips. "I don't know."

She looks out the window next to my bed, and is still. My

brother has quieted against her chest.

I want to look outside to see whatever Grandma is looking at, but then she turns to me again, her voice soft.

"Does he ever hurt you guys?"

She's asked me this before.

The first time Momma hid us was when I was very little. My sister was a baby, and Momma put us in her closet. There were slats in the door, and Daddy came in. Momma sat on the bed and put up her hands, and Daddy took the lamp on the bedside table and brought it down over her head.

"Does he ever hit your mother?" Grandma asks.

I bite my tongue.

I wasn't supposed to have seen.

"Yes."

I expect Grandma to be angry, but she's just quiet as she looks past me, her eyes softening as they stare at the wall behind my bed. She already knew. I didn't have to tell her.

"I don't want him to come back, either," I say.

My words break her gaze, and she looks back to me, her brows furrowing.

"Your dad," she starts. "He's—"

"Like her?" I ask, then hold my breath when she looks at me strangely. "Like his mom?"

She's quiet a moment as she stares at me, then looks down.

"Yeah," she says. "That's what I'm afraid of."

"Did you know her?"

"I met her once," she says. "It was after all that stuff happened, and she was getting better, but there was something about her." She looks back up. "Something that just wasn't right."

I am afraid to ask anything more, about what Grandma knows, and what I don't, so I stop talking, and Grandma tells me goodnight.

I can't stop thinking about her, and when I sleep, I dream that Daddy comes. He's angry, and he paces my room. He sits down on my bed and tells my sister and me to get in a line.

I feel his hands on me, and I look up at him.

But his face is not there.

It's Daddy's momma's face.

I wake up sweating, my covers strewn. My brother's crying in the other room.

I'm cold, and my pajamas feel wet. I reach down to touch where it feels damp, and my hands come away dark. Blood.

Forty-one

Momma hears me in the bathroom and comes in, but doesn't seem surprised at my bloody pajamas, the pink water in the sink as I try to scrub them clean. She motions me to the bathtub as she takes the pajamas from me, draws a bath, and talks quietly of things she says I need to know, ones she calls woman things.

She says my body can have babies now, is getting ready to be a wife, mother when I am older. She gets a piece of paper and a pen and starts to draw something for me, and I think she will draw me and what is happening inside, so that I can understand, but she draws stick figures, each one a different size.

Her hands are wet and the ink smears, but she points out who each stick figure is. Daddy's form is tall, his head big, and Momma draws herself next to him, shorter and with long hair. She draws my sister, then my brother is littlest of all. She draws a figure away from them, one taller than my sister, but with long hair like Momma's, and I know that it's me.

"At a certain time in everyone's life, a person reaches an age where you decide how you are going to live your life," she says. "You are that age now, tonight."

She draws thunderclouds overhead, then a big umbrella over Daddy and my family, a little umbrella over me.

"Now, you are on your own," she says. "And your family can't protect you anymore."

She says that God sees what I decide, and will pass judgment if I don't follow Him.

She draws the clouds bigger, darker, and makes more raindrops coming down. They miss the big umbrella over my family and hit me instead. My umbrella isn't strong and falls through. The rain comes more and takes over me, long lines she draws up and down my body, the ink smearing again until I can't tell what or who was there before.

"You see?" she asks.

I nod, and she puts the drawing away, pulls a towel off the rack, and holds it out to me. She gets me new pajamas and after she puts new sheets on the bed, she covers me up, and kisses me good night.

When she leaves, I look out the window and search for the thunderclouds Momma drew, and they are everywhere. There's no rain—there hasn't been rain in weeks—but the clouds are dark without the sun, and I can't see the stars.

When we looked at the stars in the mountains, Momma pointed out the North Star, said we could use the stars as a map to guide us home if we were lost, but tonight, I don't see it. I don't see any of the stars or the moon or any light in the sky at all.

Forty-two

The clouds are gone on Momma's birthday, and Grandma makes a picnic lunch, and we sit on a blanket in the front yard. Grandma brings out lemonade she pours in little plastic cups and sandwiches made of peanut butter and honey, ones cut in fourths so that they are miniature triangles, and we eat on the grass.

My sister and I give Momma our gifts first, ones Grandma helped us wrap in green paper that she tied with ribbon. Her writing is on each one—from my sister, a new Bible cover, from me, a compact mirror, and one from my brother, a box with a blue container of the face lotion she likes. We got them last week. Grandma bought them for us to give to her.

Momma opens the presents one by one with one hand, the other holding my brother who is asleep, then when she sees what the gifts are, kisses us, and tells us that she loves each thing. Grandma goes last and gives her a small box wrapped in green paper, too, but we don't know what this one is—Grandma wrapped it before she wrapped ours.

It's a stationery set with paper and envelopes, white ones with a design across the top with loopy letters that spell her name. Underneath is Grandma's address.

Momma sighs, and doesn't kiss Grandma as she did us.

She used to have a set like this one in the house before the mountains, one with the same design and shiny print, but with our old address, and her name next to Daddy's.

"It could be a good thing," says Grandma. "A fresh start."

She sets the stationary down.

"We can't stay forever," Momma says, and she's sad when she says this. Grandma takes her hand.

"Yes, you can," she says. "We'll be our own family."

Momma gathers the wrapping paper and starts to clean up.

"A new family," says Grandma. "Just us."

I want to tell Momma that we can stay. We like it here, but I know Momma will say no.

Momma doesn't answer Grandma, and we all help clean up. Grandma gathers the gifts, the stationary on top, and Momma's name and Grandma's address reflect in the sun.

"It'll be good for you, for them," says Grandma, and she nods to us.

Momma goes inside.

We help Grandma wash the dishes, and she and Momma don't talk for the rest of the day. That night, Daddy calls again, and they talk on the phone for a long time.

I try to listen, but Momma talks quietly, and she doesn't cry as she did before. I fall asleep to the sound of her talking, and in the morning, she's kneeling by my bed. She's dressed. She smells of the lotion we gave her yesterday.

She whispers to me.

"I have to leave for a little while," she says. "Daddy got a car. He's coming to see us, but I'm going to go away with him first so we can talk." She pets my head. "He said he misses you."

"Does Grandma know?" I ask her.

"No," she says.

Momma is quiet as her fingers go through my hair.

"Are you going to tell her?"

"Not yet." Her voice is low, the way it gets when she's thinking. "Grandma wants different things than we do. She doesn't—"

Her fingers pause on my head. "She doesn't understand our family."

I put up a hand to touch hers on my head. She moves to pet my head again, but I hold her fingers in mine.

"No, Momma," I say. "She does."

FORTY-THREE

Momma meets him outside in the night, and she's gone all day and the next night, and Grandma takes off work and stays with us at home. I take care of my brother, and Grandma helps, and when he's asleep, she reads to us before bed. It's a different book tonight, one she brings out from the closet, a book Momma had when she was a little girl.

It's of the stars, and Grandma says she used to read it to her before Momma found the stars in the sky with her father out in the yard. The pages are worn, and I know Grandma read it to her many times.

There are pictures of them, the constellations and the gods they're named after, and Grandma tells us about the stars Momma never told us about in her stories. She shows us Pegasus, a wild creature who Bellerophon tried to tame, tried to ride to the top of Mount Olympus to live with the gods, and the horse is beautiful, muscles strong as he throws his rider and gallops away.

"He was free," says Grandma, tracing his hooves and wings as he flees the mountain and his fallen rider. The drawing of Bellerophon is angry, mouth open, in his hands the bridle with which he tried to tame the wild beast. On the bridle's bit is blood, blood we also see on Pegasus's mouth as he flees, but the creature's body is untouched, the saddle also thrown, on his back nothing but wind now.

"No one could tame him," says Grandma, and she tells us of how we can still see him running in the sky if we know where to look, where he is still free.

We tell her the stories we know, of Perseus, the man with a fist whose drawing we still have, and of Andromeda, his love, who he rescues from the monster of the sea. We tell her about Cassiopeia, and Grandma fills in the gaps in our stories, shares the things Momma never said.

She finds the chapter about Cepheus—not a tilted house, but a king—one who chained his daughter to the sea for the monster he knew waited for her. Some of the story, we know, of Perseus who rescues her, but the rest is new—the wedding where Perseus has to fight for Andromeda, where he takes his weapon, Medusa's head, and turns everyone into stone.

We are quiet as the chapter ends.

"Did they get away?" I ask, and Grandma nods, and points out the window to where they are in the sky.

At first, I don't see them, and I put up my hand to follow hers, and my sister does, too, until we both see them together, then Grandma lets her hand come back down, then we do the same.

She tells us they stayed in love, were happy, and had a daughter and seven sons.

"I like that story," says my sister.

"I do, too."

FORTY-FOUR

The next morning, Grandma takes us to the kitchen where we spend all day. She looks out the window often, and when she doesn't see what she's looking for, she looks at us, kisses our noses and calls us pretty names.

She teaches us to make sun catchers out of wax, ones that Grandma teaches kids to make when teachers invite her to schools, and she gives us little metal frames to choose from, pours piles of wax crystals in each one until we've made a baking tray full of butterflies and birds. My sister's ones are the messiest, colors spilled all over the frame and mixed together, but they turn out to be the most beautiful when Grandma pulls them out of the oven, because they look like rainbows.

We watch them dry on the kitchen counter, pools of reds, oranges, and blues bubbling then settling down, and Grandma gives us ribbon to cut and tie through them. She shows us knots, the same ones we use to tie our shoes, and as we are finishing the last ones, Momma and Daddy come in the driveway.

We look out the window and see a white car with them inside. It has tinted windows and shiny black wheels. Daddy's in the driver's seat. Grandma makes a noise behind us and puts a hand over her mouth, and my sister and I get up to run outside.

Momma is happy and hugs my sister and me, then motions us toward Daddy.

Grandma watches, arms crossed, as she follows us outside.

Her eyes fill.

Momma doesn't seem to see as she kneels and points to Daddy and the car.

"Can you believe it?" she asks. "Brand new."

She stands to face Grandma. "No money down. They just let him drive it off the lot."

Daddy motions us over and talks like he does when he's happy, like a game show host, his words loud and long, and Momma motions for us to cheer after he speaks. Daddy's hands go up with the volume of his voice.

"Did you miss me?"

My sister cheers.

"I said, did you miss me?"

Grandma uncrosses her arms and rolls her eyes.

Daddy shows us inside, and the car is huge, its large seats soft, almost oily from the spray the dealership put on to protect the car from stains. He points out the cup holders, the storage space, and the extra seats we didn't have in our old van, and my sister cheers with each new thing he shows us, cheers again when he asks if we want to go for a ride.

I lean toward Grandma and try to make myself very small. I want to stay.

But he sees me, and motions me over. He's left the car on, and the air conditioner works in this one, so much more than our van did before Daddy sold it, and it's cold when we climb in. Momma stays home with Grandma, and Daddy drives us past the neighbor's houses, rolls down the windows, and blares the radio music loud, so that it rattles the speakers. My sister feels it where she's sitting in the front seat, and she looks over to where Daddy's dancing in his seat, his hands moving to his head, his arms pointing every which way, and it makes her laugh.

He gets on the freeway, and the wind that comes through the windows makes the music harder to hear, but I can feel the beats of it rattle me, moving through my seat and up my body until everything feels strange. We pass by the cow farms, the fairgrounds where people take long trailers full of horses, and when we reach the city limits, the clouds clear and we can see everything, even the mountain that Grandma says was a volcano long ago—one we've only seen pictures of until now, the clouds always covering it.

My sister's dancing, and she copies the moves Daddy makes, lifts her hands up in the air, waves them over her head like he does, and he pushes the car faster, until everything, the entire world, flies by as he closes his eyes and lets go of the wheel.

Forty-five

We get back late, and Momma moves my brother's crib to the den, so Daddy can sleep in her room. He looks at my brother as Momma does this, but doesn't touch him. Momma kneels next to the crib, and looks to Daddy.

"Isn't he beautiful?"

Daddy looks at the baby, then at her, but doesn't say anything or touch him when Momma tells him about the baby's soft skin, his downy head, and the way his brow looks like Daddy's.

As she puts us to bed, Momma asks us questions that I don't want to answer, if we missed Daddy, if we're happy that he's here.

I think of the pillow and blankets Momma's brought to the couch, so she can sleep next to my brother and leave Daddy alone to sleep. I wonder if she did the same thing when we were babies.

"Are we leaving here?" I ask. Daddy talked about taking us away on the drive today, somewhere new where we'd be a real family. He didn't say where it was.

Momma hugs us then turns out the light.

Grandma cooks breakfast for us the next morning, pancakes and eggs, but Daddy comes in our room before she calls us to eat, puts a finger to his mouth as he herds us to the front door.

"I have a surprise for you," he whispers.

He's smiling, and he makes exaggerated motions as if he's

tip-toeing, so Grandma doesn't hear him. My sister laughs and covers her mouth as she tries to be quiet. Momma sees us and waves, meets us at the door where she gives us our shoes.

She tells us goodbye, and Daddy hurries us out the door.

I don't know where we're going, but it's far away as Daddy drives south, and we pass by all the cow fields and then, there is nothing except forests and wildlife refuges. Daddy talks to us as he drives and says there's more snow on the mountain now, Daddy's sister is still working at the hotel, and my cousin is in a new play. He doesn't know the play, but I remember my cousin reading the script before we left, practicing for the part she wanted. The teacher in *The Miracle Worker*.

Daddy turns onto a gravel road, and he points out a river, one that is fed by snow that's melted from the mountains. He and Momma used to come here before we were born, he says.

We get out, and there's a trail by the river, one that overlooks it and the city beyond. It's chilly by the water. We get to a drop-off point where Daddy tells us people get in rafts and kayaks and float down the river. We don't see them on the river today. They won't be on the river for months, he says, it's too cold.

Daddy takes off his shoes and wades in with all of his clothes still on, shoulders hunching as he turns around toward us still on the shore, his mouth open, frozen around the word, *cold.* We mirror him, holding our fists tight to our bodies, shoulders hunched, as we take off our shoes, go in after him, too.

The water goes to our knees and Daddy dives down, combs through the rocks under our feet and his hands come back up with rocks, on them veins of gold.

He gives one to each of us, and we watch the brassy lines in the rock shine in the sunlight.

"Is it real?" my sister asks.

"No," says Daddy. "It's fool's gold."

He puts the rocks on the shore, takes my hand, and pulls me into the water where I can't touch the bottom. The water is freezing, and I pull back, my clothes wet and heavy with the water's weight. Daddy laughs and tells me to relax.

"Where are we going?" I ask. My sister watches me from the shore, and Daddy waves, says it will be her turn next.

"It'll be fun," he says, and I feel his arms beneath me, holding me up, as he moves deeper still.

He takes my arm, twists, and in one motion, I'm on my back, my face to the sky. I try to turn over, to reach for him, but he keeps me there, one hand still on my wrist, the other under my back, and the water covers all of me but my face.

I can't hear myself or him, only the water moving past, a continuous shushing, full and deep. I know that there are fish and water snakes in the river, and I'm tense when I move, afraid I'll touch something in the water I can't see. Daddy looks at me, puts a hand to his chest, opens his mouth, and leans his head back, his shoulders, chest rising. He's telling me to breathe.

I open my mouth for air, look up and see the sky, a flock of white birds overhead. "Homing pigeons," he called them as we drove to the river. "People take them to the valley and release them," said Daddy, "and the birds follow them back. Sometimes, they beat their masters home."

He points to them, and I can feel the vibrations of his voice through his hand. I close my eyes, breathe in, and the cold is less biting than it was before. I smell the damp earth, red clay on the riverbanks, and the yellow dust on the pine trees, everything Daddy says guides these birds home.

FORTY-SIX

I want to tell Grandma about the river and the fool's gold when she takes us to our rooms before we go to bed, but Daddy comes in then, too, waves her out. "I got this," he says, and Grandma puts her hands up and walks out the door.

He's never put us to bed before, and we stare at him awkwardly as he looks for a place to sit. Momma usually kneels by the bed, Grandma, too, but Daddy moves the lamp and sits on the nightstand. We take our places in our beds.

"You want a story?" he asks, and my sister brings out our books, the one of women from the Bible and the one Grandma gave us about the stars. We aren't finished with Grandma's book yet, and I take it and give it to him. I show him where we are, and we tell him of the stories Grandma already told us, of the horse that got away, the lovers who escaped from the king who was also a house made of stars.

Daddy looks bored, and he sighs dramatically. He takes the book from us and turns to the back where the pages are white. "How about I tell you a new story?"

He gets out a pen from his pocket and starts to draw, and my legs curl up against my body. His scrawl is bigger as he scratches his first drawing out and starts again.

"We're going to build a new house," he says, and he draws the house for us, complete with multiple stories and rooms and more rooms that he keeps adding on. It becomes so big, it doesn't look like a house at all. I fight not to cry. He's ruining the book.

My sister asks him how he knows the way to build a house, and he says he knows lots of things.

"We'll get away from here," he says. "And we'll all build a house together. I'll make the frame and pour the foundation." He makes the motions with his hands and draws them on the page. He colors in the doors and the windows, and the ink starts to smear.

"But how will you get these things?" I ask. "Houses cost a lot of money to build."

He stops drawing and looks at me. He clenches his jaw and closes the book. Standing, he gives it to me before he walks out the door. My brother is crying in the den.

I turn to the page where Daddy drew the house and the ink has smeared on the following blank page, ruining that one, too. The house is crooked and ugly.

I tear it out, and when I go to the kitchen to throw it in the trash can, I see what else has been thrown away. Pictures Grandma took of us when we left the mountains and came here, the pink washcloths she left on our pillows, and Momma's birthday presents. Her stationary is covered in coffee grounds, and each sheet of paper is ripped into tiny pieces until there is nothing left of Momma's name or the address beneath it.

FORTY-SEVEN

Daddy waits until Grandma is working at the screen shop before he throws away more, and I tell my sister we'll play Hide and Seek, and then I hide in the kitchen, in the cabinet where Grandma keeps her pots and pans. I move them first, way into the back, so I can fit, and I keep the cabinet door cracked until he comes in.

He takes the pictures on the refrigerator, of us smiling with Grandma at Christmas, holding up our pajamas, all matching, and Daddy rips those pictures up, too. Those are harder to rip, but he's strong, and he stuffs them all down the trash can, covers everything with paper towels and pours coffee over them until everything blends together.

He takes the trash outside, and I imagine that it steams in the bin where he's thrown it.

My brother has been crying more than he usually does, and Grandma brought home medicine for fevers, but from my spot in the cabinet, I see Daddy throw that away, too.

He looks for my book of stars, but I've hidden it.

It's in the chest of old clothes where we used to play with Grandma in the garage.

I get up early the next morning to make sure the book is still there, and Grandma is by the chest, dressing for another children's party later that day. She has her costume hanging up, freshly ironed, and her make-up kit is out. She smiles and waves me over, and I hug her, holding onto her for a long time.

My brother cries in the den. I know Daddy will wake up soon.

"Take me with you," I say, and she kneels down, her eyes sad.

"I wish I could," she says. "Your dad wouldn't like it."

I sit on her knelt knee even though I'm too big for it. I hug her close and smell her. She's fresh, her hair still wet from the shower.

"I miss you," I say.

"I miss you, too," says Grandma. "I'm sad for you guys, for your mom."

She looks past me to where Momma is sleeping on the couch. "I know she loves your dad. I just wish better for her."

Momma stirs as my brother starts to cough and makes more noises from the crib.

"I think she wants to be strong by staying with him," says Grandma. "In a way, I guess, she thinks she's being brave."

I think of the way Momma looks at him, happy and sad, at the same time. Yesterday, she and Grandma watched Daddy play with my sister in the yard, chasing her, then grabbing her tight, throwing her in air as she screamed before he caught and brought her back down her to the ground.

Momma nudged Grandma then. "See?" she asked. "He's trying."

But Grandma didn't say anything. She watched them, arms crossed, then went inside and slammed the door.

FORTY-EIGHT

My brother doesn't sleep all night and coughs between cries, making sounds that seem strange from a baby, his face red, whitening only when he gasps for a breath. Daddy's in the living room, the TV turned up loud, and he turns it louder as my brother starts to scream. Momma's holding him, but he won't be quiet, and she looks up the ceiling and closes her eyes.

Grandma comes back early from the screen shop. In her hands is a bag from the pharmacy. The TV is very loud now, so much I feel the sounds in my feet and in the walls when I touch them. Grandma covers her ears when she comes inside and heads to the TV. She turns it off.

Daddy's on his feet and behind her in seconds.

He says her name, and it sends chills through my body. He's never said any of our names like that.

Grandma ignores him and heads to Momma, gets out what's in her bag.

"I can't believe he's still like that," she says, and she opens the box of medicine. "He needs to go to the doctor."

Momma looks to Daddy. She's seen the trash cans, too.

Grandma pulls out the bottle and hands it to Momma, but Daddy's there. He steps between them and takes the bottle away.

"He needs that," she says.

Daddy's voice is low. "Not from you."

He walks away, medicine in hand.

Grandma follows him to the kitchen where he throws the bottle in the trash can. "What are you doing?"

She's angry now, and she fishes the bottle out again.

And that is when she sees everything else. Pictures. My brother's clothes. The other medicine she brought home before.

"What is this?" She asks under her breath, mouth clicking each time she finds something new.

She pulls things out until everything is on the floor. She goes outside, and I hear her yell. She's found the other bags. Our clothes, Momma's stationary.

When she comes back in, she scares me. I've never seen her so angry, her lips tense, her eyes narrowed, her voice growly.

"That is it," she says, and she takes the bottle of medicine again, opens it and dips the medicine dripper in, makes it full. She goes to my brother where he is still screaming in Momma's arms.

I'm in the doorway. My sister comes up behind me.

My brother shrieks.

"No," says Momma.

"Move," says Grandma, and she pushes Momma's hand away and puts the medicine dispenser to my brother's mouth, but her hand flings to the side, the medicine splattering on the floor.

My brother shrieks again.

Daddy's behind her, and he backs her to the wall.

Momma pulls at him. Grandma's screaming now.

My sister starts to cry.

"You're crazy," screams Grandma, and she pushes Daddy

back.

He doesn't budge, but continues to back her up until she can't move. She pushes against him, hard.

His hand clench at his sides.

She pushes him again.

"You're fucked in the head," she says, hitting her own forehead with her hand. "Just like your mother."

Daddy takes in a breath, ready to strike her, and that's when I do it.

I grab the closest thing to me and hurl it toward him. A lamp.

It bounces off him and tumbles to the floor.

Glass flies everywhere.

For a second, everyone quiets.

Daddy slowly turns, then looks at the glass on the floor.

I suddenly feel shaky.

I stumble back.

"I'm sorry," I whisper.

His eyes narrow on mine.

I feel my breath whoosh from my body.

I'm in the air.

Daddy has me, and I only see a whirl of ceiling, glimpses of Grandma running behind us until we are in my room.

Daddy locks the door.

He throws me down.

Grandma is screaming outside. "Goddamn, you," she says. "Goddamn, you," she says again and again.

Daddy takes me by the hair, and his fist slams my side.

150

"Please," I scream at him. "No, Daddy, please."

I fall to the ground, and he's on top of me. His fist smashes my face.

I scream at him again, and he puts his hand over my mouth, so I can't breath. I can't see. Blood is in my eyes.

I sign to him. "No," my right hand says, close to his face.

I sign again, and he catches my hand with his, moving his off my mouth, so I can breathe.

"Please, Daddy," I say. "I'm sorry."

I sign *sorry*, a fist rubbing a circle over my chest, and he takes my hand mid-sign.

I feel the heat of his skin. He clutches my fingers, opens my fist, and I feel his breath. His eyes meet mine. I've never been this close to his face.

"I know," he says.

He blinks, and my fingers bend back.

He snaps them hard, back where they shouldn't bend, and I feel my fingers break.

And beyond that, I remember nothing.

Forty-nine

Momma and Grandma are over me. I don't feel anything, and their voices sound as if they are coming from dreams, distorted and somewhere far away, but I remember what Grandma says.

"I'll kill him," she says. "I swear to God, I'll kill him," and I know she's talking about Daddy.

I don't know where Daddy is, because I'm asleep again, and when I wake up, it is almost morning.

I'm in the car, and Momma's buckling me in. Daddy's in the driver's seat, and my sister and brother are already strapped in. The houses on the street are dark. Momma puts her face down close to mine.

"We have to leave now," she says, and I look for Grandma, but I don't see her anywhere.

Momma closes the door.

I'm lying down in the seat, and it's hard to see outside. I'm in different clothes. My hand is wrapped. Bags of ice are on my ribs. A blanket covers my legs, and everything hurts, so I keep still.

We back out of the driveway, and I see only the top of the window, the sky overhead, and it's dark from these new windows, the ones tinted, so no one can see in. I don't know where we are going, but I feel the car turning, then going faster beneath me.

It's quiet for a long time, and I hear only the coughing of

my brother. We stop twice at gas stations where Daddy fills the car with gas and then we leave again, and late in the day, I look out at the horizon where the sun is beginning to set.

I see the mountains, the ones we left so long ago, and for a moment, I am happy that we are going back, until I watch them come close, then pass by. The snow is gone now, the trees bare and ugly, and I imagine what I know is at the top, the lake by the slopes, the houses whose chimneys give up plumes of smoke, and Daddy's sister's house at the end of the lane behind a black oak tree.

The mountains grow small, smaller than I ever remember them as we drive away toward the desert, and when they are gone, I look up at the sky again, and some of it is turning to night, the stars barely there.

I see ones I haven't seen in a long time and when I see Cepheus, I lift my hand to tell my sister, but I can't reach her. The house of stars is barely there, and I count the stars in the constellation to make sure it's the one I think I see. It is. It hangs in the sky, tilted down like it always is, and I watch it until that, too, is gone.

FIFTY

It is dark when we stop again, and when I lift my head to the window, dozens of semi-trucks are parked in rows, their large windshields reflecting the streetlights overhead. We're at a truck stop, and Momma opens the car door and tells us to get outside.

I sit up, the first time I move all day, and the bags that Momma's filled with ice roll off me. They are melted now, and Momma takes them and throws them away.

Everything hurts still, and I have to take small breaths. It's better when I hold my breath, so I do this as long as I can when I step out of the car. Momma picks up my brother, and I follow her and my sister to the market inside the gas station. Daddy stays outside.

We go to the back where the bathrooms are, and Momma hurries us all inside and locks the door behind us. My sister goes to the bathroom first as Momma changes my brother on the floor.

A mirror rests on the wall above the sink, and I stare at the girl who looks back at me.

I don't recognize myself.

My hair is straggly. My face is bruised, and I touch it as I step toward the mirror, leaning over the sink, inches from the glass. The side of my head is sticky where there is dried blood, and my cheek is puffy and colored. I feel over my body where other places hurt, show them to the mirror and see more bruises until I think to lift my shirt.

I do it slowly, afraid of what I will see.

My skin looks strange, a map of reds and purples that start at my back and branch over to my side. I forget to hold my breath, and when I breathe, I feel the marks, a new kind of hurt, deep and sharp in my body.

Momma comes up behind me, and I feel her hands take my shirt and pull it back down. I look at her, at my sister who is now staring at me, but we don't say anything as Momma turns on the water and motions for us to wash our hands.

I pause, still looking in the mirror, and Momma puts my own hands under the water with one of hers, wipes on soap, puts them under the water again and tears out paper from the dispenser before drying my hands off, one after the other.

She's never done this before, and I feel like a child.

She unlocks the door, moves us close to her with her free hand as she holds my brother with the other, and we walk back outside. Momma opens the car door, and we all get in.

When I lie back down again, I realize I never used the bathroom. I forgot in front of the mirror.

I touch my head and pick at the blood that crusted there, break the scabs down and pull them down the strands of my hair. I try to remember, but I can't.

It's a black space.

FIFTY-ONE

When we stop again, we're at a Wal-Mart. Daddy stays in the car, and everyone else gets out, but when I unbuckle my seatbelt, Momma holds me back.

"You stay here," she says.

I look at her, then to Daddy still in the front seat. I know why she wants me to stay. My face and my bandaged fingers.

"I want to go with you."

Momma shuts the door. "We'll be right back."

She carries my brother toward the front of the store. My sister strides beside her.

The car is hot already, and I lean my head against the window, and feel the warm glass against my skin. The parking lot is busier than some of the others where we've stopped, and I watch the families unload their shopping carts, close their doors, and drive away as other cars take their place, and the process begins again.

Everything is quiet in the car, and I check to see if Daddy's asleep, but he's awake, staring out to the parking spaces ahead of him. I stare at the rearview mirror to see his face, the hard lines of his nose and his lips. I know he won't look back at me. He hasn't said a word to me, to any of us, since we left Grandma's.

The door opens, and my sister jumps in. She and Momma are carrying bags, and as Momma puts my brother in the car, my sister unpacks the bags one by one, showing everything they bought inside, drinks, snacks, and diapers. She saves one bag for last, and when she opens it, she pulls out a stuffed kangaroo, a toy that's young for her, but one with a pouch she uses like a purse. She puts everything she has—a hairclip, a nickel and two pennies—inside.

There is something left in the last bag that she took the kangaroo from, and she hands it to me. I look inside. It's a notebook.

"I got that for you," she signs. "It's one with lines."

I pull out the yellow spiral notebook and open it up. It's on college-ruled paper and separated into sections.

"I told Momma you wanted to draw," she signs, a lie.

She knows why the papers mean so much to me. The letters my cousin and I used to write to each other in the mountains, the drawing of the telephone that my cousin drew that would bring the police there. I signed to my sister before we went to sleep that I needed to write these letters again.

"Thank you."

I lean over to her, so she can't see that she's made me cry. I hold her against me, and she hugs me back, careful not to touch where she knows I still hurt.

"I love it," I sign when I pull away, and she stares at the way I make the words one-handed with my good hand.

She smiles as she nods, hands me a packet of two pens, and I take them, too. My broken hand aches as I move it, and I pull back the wrapping to see my skin beneath. Two fingers are propped straight with popsicle sticks, taped down tight, the skin all around is black and dark purple. I don't remember Momma straightening them.

My sister helps me unwrap the pens as we pull back onto the freeway.

It's the fingers on my right hand that are broken, my writing hand, so I write with my left, and the letters are shaky and hard to draw. I take note of the signs we are passing now, the cities I've never seen along the 40 that goes across the whole country. I write down their names, Albuquerque, Santa Rosa, and Amarillo, how many miles left to get to the next city, and write those down, too. I write about the places we've already been. I write this all to Grandma.

Fifty-two

The first hotel we stay at is one Daddy finds in the dark when most of us are asleep, one by the interstate next to a building painted pink and whose windows are blacked out. The building's neon sign has an outline of a woman's crossed legs, and she's wearing high heels. Momma tells me to cover my eyes, says that it's a bad place.

She walks into the hotel to ask for a room, and when she's inside, I uncover my eyes and look at the pink building again. The walls are plain, and the building looks simple except for the railing that leads up the front steps. A man comes outside, and the door closes behind him, and that is when I hear the faint beat of music. It's music I don't know.

I write about the pink building and the sign of a woman's legs when we get inside the hotel room, and Daddy puts the news on. Momma doesn't tell me to go to sleep, so I write more until I can't keep my eyes open anymore. I write about the hotel and the way the air conditioner in the window clatters when someone turns it on, the Wal-Mart where my sister got a kangaroo and brought me a notebook filled with lined pages, the credit card Daddy uses to pay for our things, and the paper Momma asks to borrow, so that she can write down how much we spent that day and how much money is left before we can't spend anymore.

I wait until the morning to tear the letter out of my notebook, fold it up as many times as I can and hide it in the room. Every time we stay in a hotel after that, I hide my letter somewhere where Momma won't find it, but someone else will—under the telephone, in the pillowcase, between the pages of the Gideon Bible in the bedside table.

In each of them, I tell Grandma that I miss her. I get sad when I think of these things, when I sign my name at the bottom, and when I hide the letters before we leave. If I'm the last one out of the room, I'll make the letter more visible, a corner poking out for someone to see, and close the door. As we drive on the next day, I think about my letters, wonder if anyone found them, and if they know how to find Grandma, because I know that somewhere, she is looking for us.

Fifty-three

I tell my sister where I put the letters after I leave them, and she tells me more places to hide them—places other than the hotels where we sleep—in the open where people will find them and know where we are. She tries to sign small, knowing that the letters are secret and motions how I can hide slips of paper in the bathroom stalls we go in at the gas stations. She signs that she can leave them for me in the places Momma still doesn't let me go—in McDonalds, Wal-Mart, and her signs get big as she gets excited and names more, and I have to stop her hands.

I don't want Momma to see.

She's asleep, so I tell my sister that yes, we will hide the letters in those places, too. She smiles, shy, and looks at her hands where I've put my own.

"Do you want me to write something for you?" I sign. "Something to tell Grandma?"

Her face becomes serious as she thinks, and she doesn't hesitate before signing again.

"Tell her that I miss her."

I write this down.

"And I miss the day we first went to her house," she signs, then smiles as she remembers. "And all the things she got us. And the whipped cream she sprayed in our mouths."

I smile and write this down, too.

My face grows hot when I think of the way Grandma laughed when she did this, the way her voice got high when she saw the way the cream missed and fell from our chins, and I have to hold my breath, so my sister doesn't see me sad. I miss these things, too.

I leave this letter in the last hotel we stay in—one with sun-blocking curtains and floral wallpaper. I'm the last person to use the bathroom at night and after I wash my face and change my clothes, I open the cabinet under the sink and look for a place to leave it. The shelves are dusty, and I pull the extra rolls of toilet paper out and peer past the pipes toward the back where the cabinet meets the wall.

But a letter is already there.

It's lodged, and I have to pull it before it comes free. I open it, and it's a drawing, a stick figure made from the hands of a young child. It's of a lone person standing up, the body long with a large circle for a face. On it, two dots make eyes and a smaller circle makes a mouth. The fingers and toes are long, too, and extend out from the hands and feet. Underneath is only one word.

"Me."

Fifty-four

Momma asks to borrow more notebook paper to write down how much money we have left to use on the card, and as she writes, the numbers in the columns grow, her script becoming larger with each entry until at the bottom of the last page, there is the final amount we can use followed by "left" in all caps, then the amount circled and underlined.

$36.74.

We park at Wal-Mart. This will be our last stop.

I give my sister my letter, and she takes it, hides it under her shirt. Her face is serious and as she and Momma walk away, I watch the way my sister holds her arms close to her body, my letter hidden against her skin.

I can see my reflection in the window. My cheek isn't puffy anymore, but still dark, my skin a haze of color. I touch the tender skin.

I see something else move in the glass.

Daddy. He's watching me in the rearview mirror.

I settle back in my seat as I stare back at him. My eyes don't leave the mirror.

I don't know what to say, and it seems that he doesn't either. He flips the switch on the mirror, one that angles it, so the headlights from the cars behind him don't hurt his eyes.

He doesn't see me anymore, and I can't decide if I am angry at him for doing this or happy. I don't want to talk to him.

The car door opens, and my sister rushes in, breathless, smiles and nods her head, and I know the letter's gone.

She told me where she would leave it, but she leans over to me as Momma gets in, too, and we head out of the parking lot. "I changed my mind," she whispers. "We had to put some stuff back, because they were too expensive, but Momma wasn't looking when we were by the register. I put it there."

Out in the open.

"I wanted to be brave," she says.

I think of what the letter said, that we started sleeping in the car at night in parking lots where there weren't many cars, that we were staying on the same road, that we were almost out of money.

I drew a line like my cousin had done in her letter to me about the telephone. A line from Grandma's house to our car and where we had gone, down the coast and then turning, so we are driving across the country. The line stopped where we were now, at the Wal-Mart in Ozark near the interstate where sometimes we could see the Arkansas River. The line then looped back to the road where I knew we would go.

Fifty-five

Momma teaches us tricks to make what we have last, and when my brother's diapers run out, she empties the plastic bag we have in the back that holds all our clothes, and takes one of her shirts, folds it again and again until it looks almost like a diaper, and she fastens it closed on my brother with pieces of duct tape we have in the glove box. She takes the empty bag and sets it under where he lies, and whenever we are at a gas station, we take extra paper towels from the bathrooms to wipe him clean as Momma washes the cloth diaper in the sink and wrings it out.

We don't run the air when we drive to use less gas, but when the gas runs low, Momma doesn't have any tricks for that, only asks us to pray. We get off the interstate and drive slow on the smaller roads. Momma starts to cry.

Daddy tells her to stop. "We're going to be okay," he says. "We'll be fine."

I want to tell Momma that we can go back, but I don't, because Momma's crying has already made Daddy angry. His breathing has started to change. No one says anything, and we drive on.

The trees are thicker here, and the air feels hot and almost wet. We see signs with backpacked stick figures and tents, and Daddy follows the signs to a gravel parking lot where several other cars are. Some have trailers and other cars have bikes strapped onto the back. It's a campground, and when we pull into the lot, the low gas alarm chimes.

Daddy turns off the car and gets out.

He doesn't say where he's going, and Momma turns around, but I already know what she's going to say. He just needs to clear his mind.

We wait for him, and it starts to rain. My sister falls asleep, and Momma starts to hum one of her worship songs.

More people come and unpack their cars. They carry coolers, tents, and sleeping bags, and head down the path where Daddy went. They all pass a bulletin board with small papers tacked on the board, and stop, look at where they want to go, then put their own papers up, too. They are too far away to read, but there are a lot of them, and I wonder what they say.

Daddy comes back up the trail. He waves to us, points down the path, and motions for us all to follow him.

I wake my sister up, and we hurry to put on our shoes and run to catch up with him.

He heads back down the trail, and we pass by the bulletin board with the papers everyone left behind.

They are names, each paper placed where the owner will camp. The trail makes a loop and papers with names dot the trail almost all the way around. There are dates on the papers, too, and they all say the same date for today.

"We'll find something here," Daddy says, and he points down the trail, past tents where people are starting to build fires.

We come across a campsite where some people have just left, and Daddy looks for things they might have left behind. We find old beer cans, empty chip bags, and several opened boxes of cookies, but not all the food is gone. Daddy takes up what's left of the cookies, the bread still left in a bag of hamburger buns, and the coke bottle still half full near the picnic bench, and we take it back to the car where we divide it up and eat it all.

It tastes good, and Daddy is happy, talking again to us in way he hasn't in a while as he smiles big and touches my sister's shoulder when he tells us how we'll live off the land here, that we'll be wilderness people, and we won't have to worry about anything.

I think of what he says when we sleep in the car that night, and I remember how he led us down the trail toward the tents. There were other trails, too, ones that led deeper into the woods, and I wonder if these places had campsites, too, and if the people there would leave more food behind.

While we were walking, I went down one whose path was thinner and not as well-tread before Momma called me back to the rest of them to follow Daddy, and I wonder what would have happened if I didn't answer, if I pretended not to hear, if I kept going and never came back.

Fifty-six

We take note of where the busy campsites are and where to go back when the campers are gone. Daddy shows us how to keep track of where we are, how to mark trees, and leave signs on the trail to keep us from getting lost. With smooth stones, he shows us how to make small towers, three rocks on top of one another, then tells us to make towers of our own.

I didn't know Daddy knew these things.

My sister asks him what else he knows, and Daddy points to plants along the trail, tells us which ones to stay away from, and points to the ground beneath him, tells us to stay close, and we do. The trail gets rockier toward the end of the day, and when the stars start to come out, Daddy points to them and shows us how to follow them.

But he's wrong.

They are hard to see through the trees, but the direction Daddy says is East is not and star he says is the North Star is not a star at all.

My sister thinks it's funny and puts a hand over her mouth.

"It's okay," Momma mouths, and moves her hand to quiet us.

I don't listen anymore then, and instead, think about what to write in my next letter to Grandma, and where to leave it, because we don't stop at the places we used to anymore. That night, I write about how we take sponge baths in the public bathrooms now, taking turns with an old shirt that we wet and rinse in the sink. I write about my brother who still cries most of the night, coughing until he can barely take a breath, and whose bottom is red now, because we don't have soap to clean his T-shirt diapers or baby powder to keep him dry. I write about the bulletin board at the beginning of the trail where the papers with names are starting to disappear.

Fifty-seven

My brother's rash starts to bleed, and Momma leaves the T-shirt diapers off to let the skin breathe. Daddy goes off to the campsites again and when he passes by the board, I wonder if he ever looks at it. The papers are gone.

There are no campers left.

Momma waits until he leaves and points to the big trash dumpster at the edge of the parking lot. "We'll look in there for things," she says.

My sister is the first one to get there, and I help her get inside before I jump in behind her. The inside is strange, everything under our feet stinking and warm, and the walls echo the noises we make turning things over. Momma stays outside and holds my brother, but peeks in and points to places for us to look.

My sister finds things better than I do, and she hands Momma a half-used roll of paper towels and a plastic wrapper with two slices of cheese inside. Momma points to the foil in the corner of the bin and tells us to pick it up. Inside is a cooked chicken breast, but we have to bat away the flies, and it feels warm and mushy in our hands.

Momma divides up the cheese and when my sister and I climb out, we eat it while Momma chews up the chicken and spits it back out, then feeds it to my brother as if he were a baby bird.

Momma catches what falls out of his mouth and feeds it to

him again, then licks her fingers for anything that is left. He eats, and Momma makes sounds with her mouth as if she's chewing to get him to do the same, and soon, everything is gone.

In the car, we wait for Daddy, but the cheese has made me hungrier, and I sign to my sister of all the things we would eat if we had all the food in the world. Ice cream, lasagna, the root beer floats Grandma used to make.

She likes this game and signs of the marshmallows she loves and the way we used to roast them on straightened coat hangers over the fireplace before eating them in the house we used to live in before the mountains. Chocolate and graham crackers, she signs, the words slow as she closes her eyes and tastes them.

I know it would make Momma sad if we played this game with her, so we don't and keep our signs for when she isn't looking, and soon the day is gone. Daddy comes back.

He has nothing.

"We'll try again tomorrow," he says, and I want to point him to the board where there are no names, tell him that tomorrow will be the same, but I don't.

It gets dark, and we go to sleep, and in the night, Momma wakes up and has to go outside. She's sick, and when she comes back and picks up my brother, we see that he is, too. He's gone all over the trash bag, soiling the seat underneath, and everything stinks as we get out and try to clean the place where he was. Momma gets sick again and leaves my brother with me, and I hold him and walk him around the lot as he cries. Daddy and my sister go back in the car, but leave the doors open to let the air in, and I walk more, but my brother gets sick again all over me until I think there must be nothing left inside of him.

I don't know how to quiet him, and I want to cry, too. I play the game I played with my sister with him, although I know he can't hear me. I play a new game just for him.

I tell him about the bottles Grandma would make him and heat in a pot on the stove. I tell him about the stuffed animals she put in his crib, the teddy bear she said was hers when she was a girl, and a block made of mirrors that Grandma showed him, so that he could see his face.

I tell him about the stars in the book Grandma gave us, and that when he is older, I will teach him these stories, too. I show him how to find the gods in the sky, looking to the horizon first, then up to the North Star. I show him the real one, not the one Daddy showed us. I point to the star in the sky.

I whisper to him. I tell him we'll follow it and find our way home.

Fifty-eight

In the morning, Momma goes off to pray and leaves us with my brother while Daddy explores the campsites. My brother's crying more today, fits that make his face red, and I try to walk with him again.

Nothing works, and he cries until he gets the hiccups, and that makes him cry more. I give him to my sister and look through the car for something that will calm him, though what I know he needs is food and medicine.

His voice is raspy, and his cries are strained, and though my sister can't hear him, she looks at me nervously as she watches me search through everything we have.

The formula is gone.

I shake out our clothes, put my fingers in the creases of the seats, look through the glove box. I don't know what I'm looking for, but it distracts me from his crying, and I don't feel as helpless when I am going through our things.

I find Momma's Bible and hold it for a moment in my hands. Usually, she takes it when she goes to pray, but she left it behind. I open it up, and papers fall out, ones she borrowed from me to write down all the costs they put on the credit card.

There is a small booklet behind these.

I open it.

It's Momma's address book, inside the addresses and phone numbers of everyone we know. I find our old neighbors,

Momma's church friends, and family members. I see the pages where Momma drew us constellations in the margins so long ago.

I flip through, and some names are crossed out where people moved and letters were sent back, and I see what will save us.

The phone number for Grandma.

I tear the page out and put the book back until everything looks as it did before.

I fold Grandma's number up and hide it in my pocket. I go to my brother who is still crying, his face wet and red, pick him up and hold him close. I lean my head to his until our skin is touching, so my sister can't read what I say. I tell him, it won't be long.

There is a pay phone down the road we passed when we first got here. I only need a few coins.

I only need to get away.

Then she'll come for us.

Fifty-nine

The next camper to visit is alone. He drives a black truck and takes out rope and a tarp from the back, and we watch him and the things he unloads—a cooler on wheels, a backpack, and a sleeping bag. He's the first camper we've seen with a beard, and he's quiet as he loads everything on his back and starts down the path. He stops at the bulletin board, takes a piece of paper, and with one hand, writes down his name.

He places it on the far edge of the trail and disappears in the trees.

Daddy talks about him all day, the way he lifted the cooler, what things must be inside, and how early the next morning, me and my sister will go with him and help Daddy take it all away.

It's raining when we do, and Daddy says that the noise will be a good distraction and help cover our tracks.

He names me the lookout, and I stay a few steps behind to alert them if anyone sees us. We go from one campsite to the next, ones that are empty now, and I count how many we have left before we reach the man we saw. Daddy didn't look at the bulletin board, but I did.

The man is four campsites ahead of us.

On our way, Daddy tells my sister what to take, his pan, all the food that he has. It's dark, and she can't read what he says, so she looks back to me.

"Take everything," I sign, making two fists, then my right

175

TAWNYSHA GREENE

hand opening and circling to encompass all Daddy wants.

She nods, and we reach it.

Daddy's quiet now, and only points, and my sister obeys. They take his pan, two packages from his cooler, and a thermos by the fire. Daddy motions for us to leave, and we do.

They rush ahead, but I stay behind a moment, leave one last letter for Grandma where they took his pan, his food, and everything else.

In it, I tell her about the campground, the things we took after the campers went away and why tonight is different, and why I feel sorry for the man, because I don't want him to be hungry, too. I draw pictures of us stealing his food and draw us as we are, our clothes dirty, our hair wild, and my fingers still broken.

I tell Grandma to come soon and sign it with my name.

Setting a rock over the letter, I pause. My sister had put the other one out in the open when she left it in Wal-Mart. I will be brave, too.

I leave the letter right in front of the man's tent where he will step out when he wakes up.

My letter shines white against the dirt. The man will find it, read it, and will know.

Sixty

The man comes back out to the parking lot the next day when Momma takes us to the bathrooms to wash. I finish first and wait for them outside, and I see him approach our car. He looks inside.

He circles the car, looking in each window. He finds where we cooked everything earlier today at the edge of the parking lot. He finds the wrappers and his pan and picks them up.

He puts the pan under his arm and pulls something out of his pocket, a piece of paper that he unfolds and reads before he looks at our car again.

My letter.

I hear Momma behind me. She's calling my sister.

The man pockets my letter and heads back down the path.

He didn't see us.

But Daddy notices the missing pan and asks us if we took it. We all shake our heads, and they talk about the man from the campsite.

"Do you think he knows?" asks Momma.

"He doesn't know who we are," Daddy says. "We're safe."

They talk into the night, and I take care of my brother while they do. His skin is pale now, his body skinny as I change him, and the rash is bleeding worse. His movements are slow, his cries quieter, and I think about how he wouldn't eat the bread Momma chewed up and tried to feed him earlier, how his eyes blink slower now.

I am hungry, but he is more so.

I hold him in the back of the car with me, and listen to Momma and Daddy talk more. The rain falling outside pelts the windows and makes their voices harder to hear.

"What are we going to do?" asks Momma, a question she's already asked before, and Daddy runs his hand through his hair and breathes out. "They're starving," she says.

He says that we'll figure it out, we'll sell things at the pawn shop and get money for food.

"What are we going to sell?"

He looks around the car, then feels his pockets.

He takes Momma's hand.

"We'll sell these," he says.

"Our wedding rings?" Momma asks.

Daddy says nothing, and she starts to cry.

He looks away, and I watch his chest move up and down as he fights to control his breathing. He holds it, then hits the steering wheel.

He turns around and nudges my sister and me, then opens the door.

"Come on," he says.

"What are you doing?" asks Momma, as he pulls me and my sister out.

"I'm fixing this," he says as he closes the door, takes us by the hands, and leads us to the dark.

Sixty-one

Daddy remembers where the campsite is, and we go straight there. The path is wet from the rain, and it's dark, but the moon is bright tonight, and I look around at the trees and the way the moon makes everything look strange in the half-light.

We reach the place, and Daddy points as he did before, makes me the lookout again.

My sister takes the pan we took last time, the cans he's left by the fire pit, and Daddy goes to the edge of the tent, finds the man's clothes and goes through his pockets.

There is a backpack near me at the edge of the campsite, one I don't remember from last time, and I stoop down. Some of the zippers are already open, and I recognize some of the man's clothes bunched up inside, the shirt he wore earlier today. I reach underneath them and feel metal, cool against my fingers. Coins.

I look down the path where we came, then to Daddy.

Daddy doesn't find what he wants, and he heads toward the cooler, picks the whole thing up.

The man hears us.

There is a shout as he opens his tent, and I clutch what coins I have, but some of them fall between my fingers. I reach my sister, grab her shirt, and drag her to the woods. I don't sound the alarm for Daddy.

In the dark, we look back at the campsite, and see a

flashlight's beam. It's on Daddy's face, and he and the man are both yelling. Daddy still has the cooler in his hands.

"What are you doing?" the man asks again and again, and Daddy throws the cooler down on the ground, and everything inside spills out.

He picks it up again and throws it at the man's chest, then moves in close to his face, the flashlight wavering as the man steps back.

Daddy raises his fist to strike him, but then man holds out something in front of him.

"I know who you are," the man yells. "I know what you're doing."

Daddy pauses, the letter thrust in his face.

"Let me help you," says the man, and my letter is lit by the flashlight. I can see us, our stick forms, and my name at the bottom

Daddy sees.

He looks back, and his eyes find me in the dark.

I run.

I hear him crashing behind me. His steps are heavy on the trail, and my sister screams as she tries to follow him. The rain comes down harder now.

The trail is slippery, and he falls and when he does, he screams my name. His voice echoes and shivers race up and down my body.

He gets back up, but when he yells again, he is farther behind me.

I take the short way back, but before I reach the gravel

parking lot, I hide in the trees, crouched low, but still moving, so I can go around. To the road.

Momma's still in the car with my brother. The car is dark.

A figure appears at the other side of the gravel parking lot. But it's not Daddy. My sister had taken the same path I did. She is looking for me.

I wave, and she sees me, looks behind her, then to me again and pushes the air with her hands. She's telling me to hide.

I hold up my fist with the coins I still have. I nod to the road. But I never told her about the phone. She doesn't know what I have in my hand.

She nods and signs to me what she thinks I'm saying to her, both hands coming to her shoulders then out in front of her.

Brave.

I catch my breath.

I sign it back, my hands touching my shoulders, then coming out in front of me until I am a mirror image of her, my hands now fists.

Sixty-two

I run until I reach pavement, and it feels odd under my feet. The coins are warm in my fist now, and I search for the public phone I know is ahead somewhere, on the left, under a streetlamp that lights the black handle, the silver cord, and the numbered keys that would connect me to her.

The phone is farther away than I remember, but when I reach it, I feed all my coins in. I can't see what they are—quarters, pennies, and dimes—but I put each one in.

I take Grandma's number from my pocket and unfold it.

I put the phone to my ear.

I dial.

I don't know what I will say, but when Grandma picks up, I don't have to say anything. Even though I stutter, when she hears my voice, she knows who I am.

She starts crying, and talks all at once, asks me where we are, where we've been.

I tell her about the letters, everything I told her in each, the campgrounds where we are, how we got food, and how we couldn't get food anymore, that we need her here.

Grandma asks me more questions, ones too fast for me to answer, then pauses.

"Do you know where you are?" she asks. "Can you tell someone how to find you?"

I can. I knew the exit number off the interstate, the turns

we took, and the name of the campground on all the signs that led us here: Dardanelle.

She tells me to call *them*, to do what my cousin told me to do in the mountains in the letter when she drew a line from our house to the police station. "They'll watch you until I can get there."

I don't say anything back. "I'm coming to get you guys," she says. "I'm coming."

I tell Grandma goodbye, and we hang up. I know the next number already.

But I don't dial it.

I hear Daddy's voice. It's down the road. He calls my name.

I dial now. Nine, one, one, then hang up. I do it again, then again.

Sixty-three

I wait in the trees out of the rain. When Daddy's voice is far away again, the phone rings by itself, something I don't remember from when I called the number in the mountains, but I don't dare pick it up. It rings again, then everything is quiet.

I don't know how long it will take for them to come.

The rain lessens, and I sit against one of the trees, my clothes already wet and sticking to my skin. The earth is cold beneath me.

I can't see what is beyond the road by the trees. It is too dark, but I remember the roads we took here and the signs for the water, and the docks where the boat rentals are. I wonder which roads they will take here, which ones Grandma will take when she comes.

I close my eyes, and smell her again. The laundry soap that smells of spring, the thick make-up she put on with a sponge when she was a clown, and her breath as she would read to us then kiss us goodnight.

We never finished that book about the stars, and I think of it still hidden in the chest in her garage. The page we last read together is marked, a story of a lion who couldn't be pierced with iron, bronze, or stone.

Our favorites are marked, too, and I imagine where the stars are above me. I open my eyes, and there is a clearing in the branches above me. I crawl under it, and lie on my back, my face to the sky.

I don't see my stars, but I know where they are.

I imagine their light behind the clouds and place them in constellations in my head, naming each star as I do. I put them where they need to be—not where Daddy said they were. The North Star. Big and Little Dippers. Cassiopeia. Andromeda. Perseus.

I trace the constellations in the sky with my fingers after each one is done.

Cepheus is last.

I remember the house of stars from the last time I saw it, tilted over on its side, and the story Grandma told me, of the king who chained his daughter to the sea.

I trace a new house of stars, except upright in a way I've never seen in the sky.

I draw each star, naming them, too, then connect them, one to the next, and make the constellation whole. It's not Cepheus anymore. There is no king here.

Inside, I picture me—a stick figure like the one in the drawing I found in the hotel, one with a body and arms and legs, and a face with a mouth. I stand alone, hands out, so they reach up and touch the walls of my house of stars, holding it up, so that it is strong.

I hear sirens in the distance.

I put my hands down and wonder if Momma and Daddy hear them, too, if they know the sirens are coming here.

I would have written about the sirens if I were to write one last letter to Grandma, the way they sounded sad as they wailed in the distance. I would have written about the constellations I made, the house, and the new places for its stars in the sky.

But I don't write these things down.

This house, these stars, I keep for me.

A HOUSE MADE OF STARS

Acknowledgements

I would like to give special thanks to my husband who patiently gave me the love and support I needed to write this book. Additionally, I owe thanks to Daniel Wallace, my editor, for his insightful advice, and to Jeni Wallace for giving this book such a warm welcome at Burlesque Press. I couldn't have asked for a better team to work with—thank you so very much.

I also owe gratitude to my writing teachers: Stephen Gresham, Judy Troy, Chantel Acevedo, Jeremy Downes, Chris Forhan, Peter Campion, Michael Knight, Allen Wier, Margaret Lazarus Dean, Thomas Turner, Richard Bausch, Marilyn Kallet, William Pitt Root, and Pamela Uschuk. My first readers who graciously gave me feedback on early drafts, thank you: Jordan Rosenfeld, Jessie Carty, Lacy Marschalk, Sandy Longhorn, and Jeremy Hager.

Thank you also to the journals and their gracious editors where excerpts (or cut sections) of this novel appeared: *Weave Magazine*, *storySouth*, *Blue Lake Review*, *JMWW*, *PANK Magazine*, *Hobart*, *Bartleby Snopes*, *A-Minor*, *Monkeybicycle*, *Waccamaw*, *Barely South Review*, *Raleigh Review*, *decomP*, *elimae*, *Dogzplot*, *Bellingham Review*, *Emprise Review*, *The Citron Review*, *Annalemma*, *Bluestem Magazine*, *Used Furniture Review*, *Necessary Fiction*, *Staccato Fiction*, *52/250 A Year of Flash*, *Eunoia Review*, *2River View*, *Wigleaf*, *The Variety Show*, *Rougarou: An Online Journal*, *Still: The Journal*, and *Cutthroat: A Journal of the Arts*.

Finally, thank you, to my family, especially my grandmother whose strength and courage still inspire me—this book is for you, Grandma.

About The Author

Tawnysha Greene received her Ph.D. from the University of Tennessee where she currently teaches fiction and poetry writing. She also serves as an assistant fiction editor for *Cutthroat: A Journal of the Arts* and is a regular reader for the *Wigleaf* Top 50 series. Her work has appeared in *PANK Magazine*, *Bellingham Review*, and *Necessary Fiction* among others.

A House Made of Stars is her first book.

CPSIA information can be obtained at www.ICGtesting.com
Printed in the USA
BVOW02s1111040815

411615BV00001B/2/P

9 780996 485005